STORY & ART BY SANTA HARUKAZE

No. 001
Central Kalos Pokémon
Chespin
Sharp Thinking

WHEN CHESPIN CONCENTRATES REALLY HARD...
...ITS QUILLS...

Quiz answer
?

Starting with page 4, you'll find the answer to the quiz from the previous page here!

po ink
...GET SHARP AND POINTY!

Stab
OWWW!

I'm sorry!
I COULDN'T HELP IT! I WAS SO INTO THE MOVIE!
Movie Theater
HMPH. I'M NEVER WATCHING A GOOD MOVIE WITH YOU AGAIN!

POKÉMON X·Y QUIZ

Chespin is so hardheaded that even a direct hit from a truck doesn't faze it. What is its head covered with?

1. A thick wood shell

2. Iron armor

3. Smooth grass

No. 002
Central Kalos Pokémon
Quilladin
Seed of Kindness

YOU'RE SO CONSIDERATE, QUILLADIN...
Heh
AW, THANKS. WHAT A NICE COMPLI-MENT.

Quiz answer for page 3.
1

Chespin's head is covered with a thick wood shell.

LOOK OUT!
bump
fweee

UM...
ARE YOU OKAY, FENNEKIN?
I WOULD BE IF I WERE A FLOWER...
QUILLADIN'S SHELL IS VERY SHOCK ABSORBENT.

POKÉMON
XY
QUIZ

What Pokémon category is Quilladin?

Spiny Nut Pokémon

Spiny Armor Pokémon

Armor Pokémon

Central Kalos Pokémon

Chesnaught

So Cool You'll Flip

BMP
CHESNAUGHT'S TACKLE IS SO POWERFUL IT CAN FLIP OVER A TANK.

OH, WOW!
LOOK AT THROH GO!

Quiz answer for page 5.

2

Quilladin is a Spiny Armor Pokémon.

IT SPUN AROUND THREE TIMES IN THE AIR AND ACED THAT LANDING.
Wff
Wff
Wff
tmp

THROH IS SO-O-O-O COOL!
WHAT ABOUT ME?! IF I HADN'T SENT THROH FLYING, IT COULDN'T HAVE DONE ANY OF THOSE AERIAL ACROBATICS!

POKÉMON X•Y QUIZ

Chesnaught attacks with Hammer Arm. Which of the following Pokémon is Hammer Arm not effective against?

1
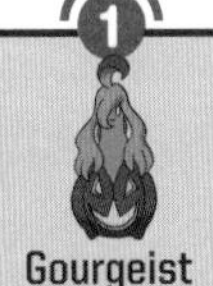
Gourgeist

2

Diggersby

3

Inkay

Central Kalos Pokémon

Fennekin

Stick to Flowers

FENNEKIN LOVES TO CHEW STICKS.
I'M HUNGRY...
I FOUND YOU A STICK! ♡

FOR FENNEKIN'S BIRTHDAY LAST YEAR...
...MY PRESENT WAS A BUNCH OF STICKS.
It's like a bouquet of sticks!
Thanks! ♡

Quiz answer for page 7.

1

Hammer Arm is a Fighting-type move, so it is not effective against Ghost-type Pokémon.

SO THIS YEAR, I USED STICKS TO...
...BUILD FENNEKIN A LITTLE HOUSE!

FENNEKIN CHEWED IT UP IN ONE-TENTH THE TIME IT TOOK ME TO BUILD IT!
THANKS! ♡
krnch krnch krnch krnch

POKÉMON X·Y QUIZ

Fennekin's Fire-type move is not very effective against which of the following Pokémon types?

1

Ice type

2

Bug type

3

Water type

Central Kalos Pokémon

Braixen

Hot and Spicy Leeks?

WHEN THE TWIG IS PLUCKED OUT OF BRAIXEN'S TAIL...
...THE FRICTION SETS IT ON FIRE.

Quiz answer for page 9.
3

Fire-type moves aren't very effective against Water-type Pokémon.

OH, THERE IT IS! ♡
My missing leek!

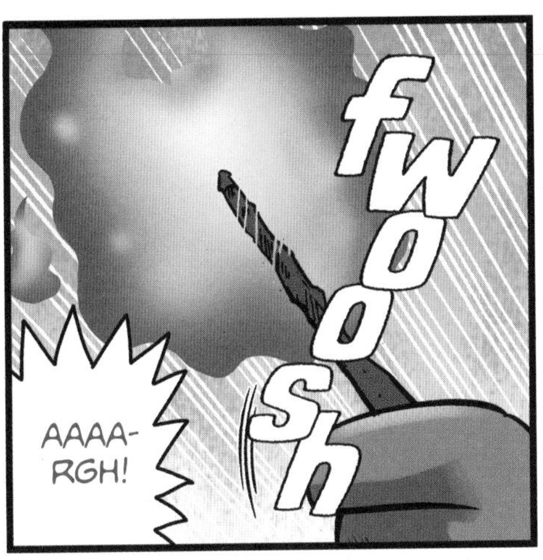
fwooSh
AAAA-
RGH!

EEEEEEEK!
MY
LEEK?!
KRCKK!
MY
TWIG?!

POKéMON
X·Y
QUIZ

Braixen uses the twig in its tail...

...to swat down flying things.

...to fish.

...as a flaming weapon in battle.

Central Kalos Pokémon

No. 006

Delphox

Illuminating Tomorrow

DELPHOX GAZES INTO THE FLAME TO ACHIEVE A ZEN-LIKE STATE, AND THEN...
...IT CAN SEE INTO THE FUTURE.
KRCKL
KRCKL

IT'S GOING TO RAIN...
...TO-MOR-ROW.
KRCKL
KRCKL

Quiz answer for page 11.

3

When plucked out of Braixen's tail, the twig catches fire.

THAT'S IT...?
THAT'S JUST A WEATHER FORE-CAST!
Hmph.

WELL, IT'S AN IMPORTANT PREDICTION FOR *ME*! BECAUSE...UM...
RAINY DAYS ARE PERFECT FOR CURLING UP WARM AND DRY AT HOME AND READING MANGA ALL DAY!
glare
Because Fire-type Pokémon hate water!

POKéMON X·Y QUIZ

What type of Pokémon is Delphox?

1

Fire type

2

Fire and Ghost type

3

Fire and Psychic type

Central Kalos Pokémon

No.
007

Froakie

No Need to Make the Bed

LOOK! I MADE A BED OUT OF BUBBLES!
bloop bloop
WOW! ♡

Quiz answer for page 13.
3

Delphox is a Fire- and Psychic-type Pokémon.

SO... COMFY... ♡
bloop
bloop
bloop
SLEEP TIGHT! ♪

MORNING...
OUCH... NOT SO COMFY...

IT WAS MADE OF BUBBLES...
grr grr grr
WHAT DID YOU EXPECT?

POKéMON XY QUIZ

Froakie attacks with Water Pulse. Which of the following Pokémon is Water Pulse super effective against?

1

Chespin

2

Marowak

3

Farfetch'd

No. 008
Central Kalos Pokémon
Frogadier
How Not to Be Attacked

OH NO! QUILLADIN IS A GRASS-TYPE POKÉMON!
I'M AT A DISAD-VANTAGE AGAINST ITS MOVES...

SO I'LL USE... BOUNCE!
boing

Quiz answer for page 15.

2

Water-type moves are super effective against Marowak, a Ground-type Pokémon.

boing
boing
boing

Let's see you battle me-up here. Nyah nyah!
NAH, I'M GOOD. THANKS.

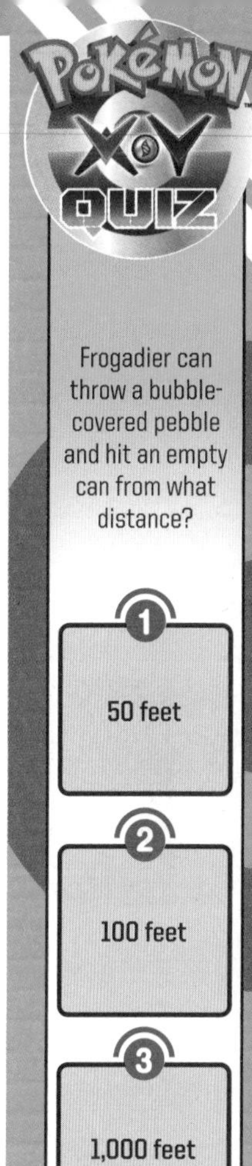
POKÉMON X•Y QUIZ

Frogadier can throw a bubble-covered pebble and hit an empty can from what distance?

1. 50 feet
2. 100 feet
3. 1,000 feet

No. 009
Central Kalos Pokémon
Greninja
Moves Like a Ninja

GRENINJA MOVES LIKE A NINJA.
ZZOOOOOOOM

Quiz answer for page 17.
2

GRENINJA MOVES SO FAST...
...IT'S A BLUR! I CAN HARDLY SEE IT!

Frogadier can hit an empty can with a bubble-covered pebble from a distance of 100 feet.

GRE-
NINJA
MOVED
SO FAST
IT...COM-
PLETELY
DISAP-
PEARED
?!
WOW

GRENINJA
IS SO-O-O-O
COOL!
WHO
DUG THIS
HOLE
HERE?!
twtch
twtch

POKéMON
X·Y
QUIZ

What Pokémon category is Greninja?

1

Hiding Pokémon

2

Sneaking Pokémon

3

Ninja Pokémon

Central Kalos Pokémon

No.
010

Bunnelby

Dig Your Way Out of This

BUNNELBY'S FAVORITE MOVE IS DIG.

Quiz answer for page 19.
3

Greninja is a Ninja Pokémon.

IT USES ITS EARS TO DIG BURROWS!
dig
dig
dig
dig

AN HOUR LATER...
BUNNELBY WON'T COME OUT OF THE HOLE IT DUG.
...
IS SOMETHING WRONG?

THAT'S WEIRD... AN HOUR AGO, BUNNELBY ASKED ME IF I WANTED TO PLAY TOGETHER.
WHAT IF FENNEKIN DOESN'T LIKE ME?!

Pokémon
X Y
QUIZ

Bunnelby attacks with Quick Attack. Which of the following Pokémon is Quick Attack not effective against?

1

Haunter

2

Diglett

3

Klefki

No. 011
Central Kalos Pokémon
Diggersby
Grandpa

HELLO, GRANDPA DIGGERSBY.

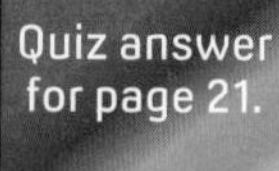
Quiz answer for page 21.

1

Normal-type moves are not effective against Ghost-type Pokémon.

I'M NOT OLD ENOUGH TO BE A GRANDPA!
I'm still young!
OH! A ROCK ROLLED DOWN AND BLOCKED THE PATH!

grab toss
DON'T WORRY, I'LL TAKE CARE OF IT!
WOW!
Thanks!

SEE? PIECE OF CAKE.
Har har har har har har
NO... PIECE OF *ROCK*! ♡
YOU MIGHT NOT BE OLD, BUT YOU STILL MAKE GRANDPA JOKES!

POKÉMON X Y QUIZ

Diggersby attacks with Mud Shot! Which of the following Pokémon is it not effective against?

1

Dugtrio

2

Staravia

3

Gastly

Central Kalos Pokémon

Fletchling

Lost in Translation

YOUR CHIRPING SOUNDS ARE A LANGUAGE, AREN'T THEY?
SURE ARE. ALLOW ME TO DEMON-STRATE.

Chirp chirpety chirp!
Chirpety chirp chirp!

Quiz answer for page 23.

2

Mud Shot is a Ground-type move. It is not effective against Flying-type Pokémon.

Chirp
Chirp
OH, LOOK! ♡ YOUR FRIENDS ARE COMING!
WHAT DID YOU SAY TO THEM?

THAT YOU'RE GOING TO DANCE FOR US. ♪
WHAT?! I CAN'T DANCE!!
Woo-hoo!

Fletchling communicates with its flock through melodious chirps and by...

...wiggling its tail feathers.

...spreading its wings.

...dancing.

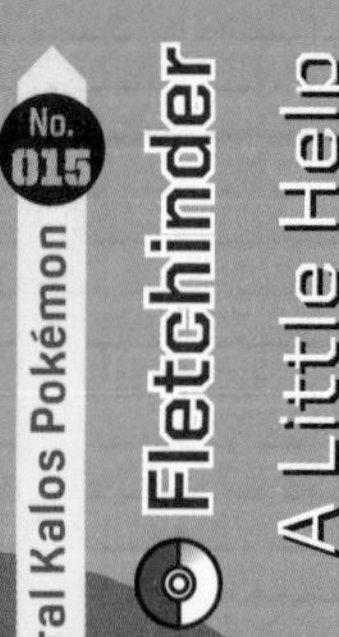

Central Kalos Pokémon No. 015

Fletchinder

A Little Help

FROAKIE, LOOK OUT!
WHAT IS IT, FLETCH-INDER?

Quiz answer for page 25.
1

fsst fsst
THERE'S SMOKE COMING UP FROM A FIRE IN THAT FIELD OVER THERE!
OH NO!

Fletchling communicates through melodious chirps and tail feather movements.

PHEW! THE FIRE'S FINALLY OUT!
WATER GUN!

GREAT. I'M GOING TO START A FIRE OVER THERE NEXT. FOLLOW ME! ♪
Wait a sec...
YOU'RE SETTING THESE FIRES?!
FLETCHINDER EXPELS EMBERS FROM ITS BEAK TO SET TALL GRASS ON FIRE SO IT CAN POUNCE ON THE BEWILDERED PREY FLEEING FROM THE FLAMES.

POKÉMON
X Y
QUIZ

What happens when the temperature of the flame sac on Fletchinder's belly rises?

It can fly faster.

2

Its Fire-type moves become stronger.

It loses its appetite.

Central Kalos Pokémon

Talonflame

Not Fast Enough

TALONFLAME ATTACKS ITS PREY AT 310 MILES PER HOUR.
WZZZZZZZZZ

A 310 MPH KICK...
KWHUMP
...HITS FAR-FETCH'D, AND...

Quiz answer for page 27.

1

The hotter the flame sac on Fletchinder's belly gets, the faster it can fly.

...ITS STALK...
...FLIES OUT OF ITS HAND AT 310 MPH AND...!
fwee

So I was like, really?!
Yeah, right!
ka thunk
310 MPH AND QUILLADIN DIDN'T EVEN NOTICE!

POKÉMON X•Y QUIZ

What happens to Talonflame when it gets excited during a battle?

It begins to attack both friend and foe.

It stops fighting.

It showers embers from the gaps between its feathers.

No. 020
Central Kalos Pokémon
Scatterbug
Comfort Food

THE POWDER THAT COVERS SCATTERBUG'S BODY...
...REGULATES ITS TEMPERATURE.
I NEVER FEEL HOT OR COLD!

Quiz answer for page 29.
3

When Talonflame gets excited, it showers embers from the gaps between its feathers.

BRR... IT'S FREEZING COLD TODAY, SCATTERBUG.
I'M NOT COLD, BUT...
...WOULD YOU SHARE THAT HOT STICKY BUN WITH ME?
fs ss

PHEW... IT'S SWELTERING HOT TODAY, SCATTERBUG.
I'M NOT HOT, BUT...
...WOULD YOU SHARE THAT COLD SOFT SERVE ICE CREAM WITH ME?

Hey, everyone! What would you like to do?!
THE WEATHER IS JUST RIGHT TODAY! LET'S PLAY!
SIGH... I WAS HOPING FOR "JUST RIGHT" TEMPERATURE SNACKS...

POKÉMON X·Y QUIZ

What happens if you come in contact with Scatterbug's powder?

1. You fall asleep.
2. You get paralyzed.
3. You start laughing.

Central Kalos Pokémon

No. 021

Spewpa

How Many Whacks Does It Take?

SPEWPA'S BODY IS...

...HARD AS A ROCK.

whack
whack
whack
whack
whack
YOUR BODY IS HARD AS A STEEL ANVIL!

Quiz answer for page 31.

2

The poisonous powder Scatterbug spews out paralyzes its opponent.

whack whack whack whack whack whack
...
YOU'RE AMAZING! DOESN'T THAT HURT?

NO. BUT IT'S STILL ANNOYING!
WHACK

POKÉMON
X Y
QUIZ

When Spewpa is attacked by a predator, it...

...bristles its fur to look bigger.

...lets out a loud cry to sound scary.

...dives into the ground to escape.

Central Kalos Pokémon

No.
022

Vivillon

A Less-Vibrant Vivillon

VIVILLON ARE FOUND ALL OVER THE WORLD AND HAVE A VARIETY OF WING PATTERNS.

HEY!

WHAT?

I HAVEN'T FORGOTTEN HOW FOOLISH YOU MADE ME LOOK IN OUR LAST BATTLE!
SORRY, YOU'VE GOT THE WRONG POKÉMON.
HAPPENS ALL THE TIME. WE VIVILLON COME IN A LOT OF DIFFERENT STYLES.

Quiz answer for page 33.

1

Spewpa bristles its fur to look big and tough.

TAKE A CLOSER LOOK... I BET MY STUNNINGLY BEAUTIFUL PATTERN IS DIFFERENT FROM THE VIVILLON YOU BATTLED.

HUH? OH YEAH...
That Vivillon was much prettier.
YEP. DEFINITELY NOT AS BLAND AND BORING AS YOUR PATTERN.
IF *MY* PATTERN IS BLAND, I'D LIKE TO SEE THE VIVILLON PANGORO FOUGHT!
SO YOU SEE, IT WASN'T ME! TOLD YOU!

QUIZ

How many patterns of Vivillon are currently known to exist?

1. 10
2. 15
3. 18

Central Kalos Pokémon

No. 023
Caterpie

Caterpie

The Only Way to Travel

CATERPIE'S FEET HAVE SUCTION CUPS THAT CLING TO ANY SURFACE.

YOU'RE A SLOW MOVER, AREN'T YOU?
I WOULDN'T SAY THAT...

Quiz answer for page 35.
3

Currently, 18 patterns of Vivillon have been identified.

…ESPECIALLY WHEN I'M CLINGING TO AN AIRPLANE!

Caterpie protects itself from attacks by...

...clinging to its enemy with its suction cup feet.

...hardening its body.

...releasing a horrible stink from the feeler on its head.

No. 047
Central Kalos Pokémon
Surskit
A Shallow Attempt at Humor

SURSKIT USUALLY LIVES IN PONDS.
THIS IS A PUDDLE.

Quiz answer for page 37.
3

THERE'S A NICE BIG BODY OF WATER OVER THERE!
SURSKIT...

Caterpie releases a horrible stink from the feeler on its head to protect itself.

I GUESS YOU DIDN'T SEE IT SINCE IT WASN'T "BAYOU."
GET IT?

urk
I GET THE MES-SAGE...
FINE. I'LL GO...
HEY, WAIT!
THERE ISN'T ANY WATER OVER THERE! I JUST COULDN'T RESIST THE PUN!

POKéMON
X Y
QUIZ

Surskit attracts its prey with a sweet scent. What part of its body does the scent emanate from?

1

Its toe

2

The tip of its head

3

The red mark below its eyes

Central Kalos Pokémon
No. 049
Magikarp
One Small Leap for Magikarp...

HUH...? ALL OF A SUDDEN I FEEL SO HEAVY...

Quiz answer for page 39.
2

Surskit draws in its prey with a sweet scent that comes out of the tip of its head.

YIKES!
HUH ?!
WHAT'S MAGIKARP DOING ON MY BACK?!

I JUMPED OUT OF THE WATER, AND SUDDENLY— HERE I WAS!
YOU ACCIDEN-TALLY JUMPED ON ME?!
OKAY, OKAY! QUIT FLOPPING AROUND!

Aaaaaaah!
What a dummy...
SOMETIMES YOU CAN MAKE A REAL SPLASH EVEN WHEN YOU DIDN'T INTEND TO.

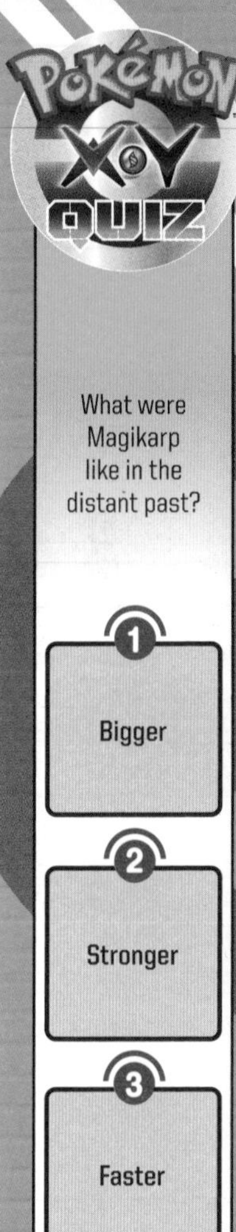
POKÉMON X•Y QUIZ
What were Magikarp like in the distant past?
1
Bigger
2
Stronger
3
Faster

Central Kalos Pokémon

Mega Gyarados
True Confessions

A MEGA GYARADOS CAN JUMP OUT OF THE WATER AT A SPEED GREATER THAN MACH 1!

ACK!

KER-SPLASH

Quiz answer for page 41.

2

Magikarp were somewhat stronger in the distant past.

YOU SCARED ME! WHY DID YOU JUMP OUT OF THE WATER LIKE THAT?!
UM...

I JUST WANTED TO GIVE YOU A KISS...
REALLY?!
AWW, THAT'S SO SWEET... I THOUGHT YOU WANTED TO EAT ME!
Shy!

POKéMON
X Y
QUIZ

When Gyarados Mega Evolves into Mega Gyarados, which Pokémon type does it change into?

Water and Dark type

Steel and Dark type

Water and Steel type

Central Kalos Pokémon

No. 054

Seaking

Falling Rocks

IN THE AUTUMN, SEAKING TENACIOUSLY TRAVELS UPRIVER AGAINST POWERFUL CURRENTS...

...DETER-MINED TO FIND A PARTNER NO MATTER WHAT.
SPISHSPISH

Quiz answer for page 43.

1

Mega Gyarados is a Water- and Dark-type Pokémon.

I GIVE UP!
CHESPIN, ON THE OTHER HAND...
...CAN'T HANDLE THE SMALLEST CHALLENGE.

A ROCK FOR PRACTICING ROCK SMASH
QUIT BEING A QUITTER!
BUT I CAN'T CRUSH IT! I JUST CAN'T!
EVEN SWIMMING *DOWNSTREAM* CAN BE TOUGH FOR CHESPIN.

POKÉMON
X Y
QUIZ

Where does Seaking nest?

Between rocks on a riverbed

Inside holes it carves in boulders in a stream

Inside holes it digs in a riverbed

Central Kalos Pokémon
No. 057
Litleo
Setting Off

HEY, EVERYONE!
I'M HEADING OUT TO LIVE ON MY OWN AND GET BIG AND STRONG!
WHEN WILD YOUNG LITLEO GROW UP, THEY LEAVE THEIR PRIDE TO FEND FOR THEMSELVES.

Quiz answer for page 45.
2

Seaking carves holes into boulders in a stream to form its nest.

UM... I'LL GO TOMOR-ROW!
WHY NOT NOW?

THERE'S NO RUSH, IS THERE?
UH... I DON'T FEEL UP TO IT AT THE MOMENT...

BESIDES, I'M SLEEPY.
ACTUALLY, THERE'S NO TIME LIKE THE PRESENT...

POKÉMON
X Y
QUIZ

What happens when a Litleo faces a powerful opponent?

1. It coats itself in poisonous vapor.
2. It pretends to be asleep.
3. Heat surges out of its mane.

No. 058
Central Kalos Pokémon
Pyroar
The Mane Qualifications

THE MALE PYROAR WITH THE LARGEST MANE BECOMES THE LEADER OF THE PRIDE.
I'M THIS PRIDE'S LEADER. ♡

Quiz answer for page 47.
3

HM... WELL, YOU CERTAINLY DO HAVE A LARGE MANE.
TOLD YOU.

The stronger Litleo's opponent is, the more heat surges out of Litleo's mane.

BUT YOU'VE GOT AWFULLY SHORT FRONT LEGS...
So what ?!
THE LENGTH OF A PYROAR'S LEGS HAS NOTHING TO DO WITH HOW THEY CHOOSE THEIR LEADER.

POKéMON XY QUIZ

Pyroar is a powerful-looking Pokémon. What category is it?

Ultimate Pokémon

Invincible Pokémon

Royal Pokémon

No.
061

Central Kalos Pokémon

Farfetch'd

Walk Softly and Carry a Big Leek

THE LEEK FARFETCH'D CARRIES AROUND MAY BE USED TO WEAVE ITS NEST.

NEST

mnch mnch

THE LEEK MAY BE EATEN AS A SNACK.

BUT MOST IMPORTANTLY, THE LEEK MAY BE USED AS A WEAPON.
Yaaahhh!

Quiz answer for page 49.
3

Pyroar is a Royal Pokémon.

ker
Eeeeek!
Smak

OR THE LEEK MAY BE USED AS A CRUTCH...
wbbl
wbbl
tnk

Which of the following is true about Farfetch'd?

Its leek can be used to catch fish.

Its leek can be used to build a place to sleep.

Some Farfetch'd carry around not one but two leeks.

Central Kalos Pokémon

Mega Lucario

The Will to Win

I FEEL ENERGY FLOWING THROUGH MY BODY!

SO THIS IS MY TRUE POWER!

Yaaahhhhhhh!

NOW I CAN DEFEAT ANYONE!

Farfetch'd uses leeks to build its nest.

I TOLD YOU, I DON'T HAVE ANY FOURS.

And how come you stood up?

Which of the following characteristics of Lucario doesn't change when it Mega Evolves?

Height

Weight

Type

No.
065

Central Kalos Pokémon

Kirlia

Premonition Problems

KIRLIA HAS THE POWER TO DISTORT SPACE AND SEE INTO THE FUTURE.

$1 per question

TELL ME WHAT'S GOING TO HAPPEN TOMORROW!

OKAY.

Quiz answer
for page 53.
3

Lucario's Pokémon type remains the same even after it Mega Evolves.

I SEE IT... I SEE YOUR FUTURE!
TOMORROW... YOU WILL PARTICIPATE IN...A BATTLE. AND THE POISON WILL...
POISON?!

THAT'S ALL.
WAIT! WHAT ABOUT THE POISON ...?!
YOU HAVEN'T TOLD ME EVERY-THING!
$1 per question

THAT'LL BE ANOTHER DOLLAR, PLEASE.
ANOTHER DOLLAR?!
A dollar per question!
I SEE YOUR FUTURE LOOKING VERY BLEAK!
$1 per question

POKéMON
X·Y
QUIZ

What does Kirlia do when it is happy?

Spins and dances

Sings

Releases fragrant flower scents

No.
066

Central Kalos Pokémon

Mega Gardevoir

Any Place in a Storm

THE GRASS FEELS SO GOOD UNDER MY FEET AFTER IT RAINS.

Quiz answer for page 55.
1

When it is happy, Kirlia spins and dances.

WHAT? THE STORM IS OVER?

THANKS. I WAS SHELTERING IN HERE FROM THE RAIN. ♪
fwap

Hyper Beam!
Eeeek!
fa-peeeew

POKÉMON
X·Y
QUIZ

Mega Gardevoir's Ability, Pixilate, has the power to...

1

...heal Mega Gardevoir when it is attacked by a Fairy-type move.

2

...double the power of its own Fairy-type move.

3

...change its Normal-type move into a Fairy-type move.

No. 068
Central Kalos Pokémon
Flabébé
Door Jammed

THE FLOWER FLABÉBÉ HOLDS IS LIKE AN EXTENSION OF ITS BODY.

ZWOOOOP
ZWOOOOP

Quiz answer for page 57.
3

Normal-type moves like Hyper Beam turn into Fairy-type moves.

ZWOOP
ZWOOP

Smash
SOMETIMES EVEN LITTLE POKÉMON...
...MISJUDGE THE CLEARANCE ON A DOORWAY..

POKÉMON
X Y
QUIZ

What does Flabébé do when it finds a flower it likes?

1

Leaves it be

2

Lives with it forever

3

Picks it to decorate its room

Central Kalos Pokémon

Floette

Tender, Loving Oops

HUH? I'VE NEVER SEEN THIS PLANT BEFORE.

GROW AND BLOOM, SWEET LITTLE PLANT!

Quiz answer for page 59.

2

Flabébé spends its entire life in the company of its favorite flower.

Eek!
jmp

DON'T DO THAT!
CAN'T I EVER SLEEP IN PEACE?!
I'M SORRY! PLEASE DON'T CRY!
IT LOOKS LIKE BONSLY IS CRYING, BUT ACTUALLY IT'S JUST ADJUSTING ITS FLUID LEVELS.

POKÉMON
X Y
QUIZ

What Pokémon category is Floette?

Single Bloom Pokémon

Flower Pokémon

Garden Pokémon

No. 070

Central Kalos Pokémon

Florges

Take My Air

FLORGES IS SO BEAUTIFUL THAT...

...IT TAKES MY AIR AWAY!
Sigh

Quiz answer for page 61.
1

Floette is a Single Bloom Pokémon. So is Flabébé.

THE WORD YOU'RE LOOKING FOR IS "BREATH-TAKING."
UM...

SO IF YOU TOOK MY DROOL AWAY... WOULD YOU BE "WATER-TAKING"?
drool drool
UM...
THAT'S A LOT OF DROOL.

POKÉMON X·Y QUIZ

What Pokémon category is Florges?

1

Single Bloom Pokémon

2

Flower Pokémon

3

Garden Pokémon

No.
082

Central Kalos Pokémon

Mega Venusaur

Good to Have a Backup Plan

ICY WIND!
fwoooosh
EMBER!

WHOA!
OUR ATTACKS HAVE NO EFFECT AGAINST VENUSAUR!
WE'VE GOT NO CHOICE! PLAN B!
?

Quiz answer for page 63.
3

Florges is a Garden Pokémon. Bellsprout is a Flower Pokémon.

WE'RE SORRY!
PLEASE FORGIVE US!

OH YEAH? ♡ WELL, NOW IT'S *PAYBACK TIME*!
IT'S NO USE! BEGGING FOR FORGIVE-NESS HAS NO EFFECT EITHER!
Plan C! Run away!

POKÉMON
X•Y
QUIZ

Mega Venusaur is not weak against Fire- or Ice-type moves. That's because...

...it has grown bigger.

...its Ability has changed to Thick Fat.

...it has grown stronger.

No. 084
Central Kalos Pokémon
Charmeleon
Chilly Reception

SHUDDER
...

Quiz answer for page 65.
2

The Thick Fat Ability halves the damage from Ice- and Fire-type moves.

CHARMELEON CAN RAISE THE TEMPERATURE AROUND IT BY SWINGING ITS FIERY TAIL.
flare
flare
flare

WHAT ARE YOU DOING ?!
HOT! HOT!
YOU WERE TREMBLING. WEREN'T YOU COLD?

I WAS SHUDDERING AT HOW TERRIBLE SLOWPOKE'S JOKES ARE!
...AND THEN THEY SAID... YOU BETTER HURRY UP, SLOW-POKE! ♡ GET IT? HUH? DO YOU?

POKÉMON X·Y QUIZ

What does Charmeleon do after defeating its enemy by swinging its fiery tail?

1

Breathes fire on its opponent

2

Steps on its opponent

3

Claws its opponent

No.
085

Central Kalos Pokémon

Mega Charizard X

The Secret of Blue

WHY ARE YOUR FLAMES BLUE, MEGA CHARIZARD X...?
ISN'T IT OBVIOUS?

Quiz answer for page 67.
3

THEY'RE BLUE BECAUSE THEY'RE MUCH HOTTER THAN BEFORE I MEGA EVOLVED.

Charmeleon scratches its opponent with its sharp claws.

SO YOUR BODY MUST BE GRAY...
OH.

MEGA EVOLVING DIDN'T RUIN MY AIM!
After all, Mega Charizard Y is red.
...BECAUSE YOU ACCI-DENTALLY SCORCHED YOURSELF, RIGHT?

POKÉMON X·Y QUIZ

Which of the following moves would be super effective against Mega Charizard X?

1

Electric-type moves

2

Ground-type moves

3

Dragon-type moves

Central Kalos Pokémon No. 085

Mega Charizard Y

Outta Sight, Outta Mind

ARE YOU WATCHING?! ♪
LOOK AT ME!
Woo-hoo!

ZWOOOM
I CAN FLY SIX MILES HIGH, SEE?!

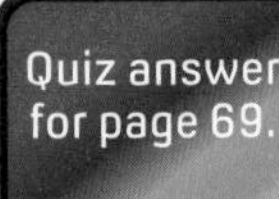

Quiz answer for page 69.

3

Mega Charizard X is a Fire- and Dragon-type Pokémon, so Dragon-type moves are super effective against it.

WHEE... ♪
AND GUESS WHAT?! I CAN FLY EVEN HIGHER THAN THIS!

BACK DOWN ON THE GROUND...
CHARIZARD DISAPPEARED. I GUESS IT WENT HOME.

POKÉMON X•Y QUIZ
When Charizard Mega Evolves into Mega Charizard Y, how many horns does it have on its head?
1
One
2
Two
3
Three

No.
086

Central Kalos Pokémon

Squirtle

How to Startle a Squirtle

GET READY...
GET SET...

BANG

Quiz answer for page 71.

3

Mega Charizard Y has three horns.

That loud sound gets me every time!
WAHHH... I LOST AGAIN!

POKÉMON XY QUIZ

Squirtle protects itself with its shell. What does it do when it attacks an opponent?

1

Hides in its shell

2

Shoots spouts of water

3

Calls its friends for help

Central Kalos Pokémon

Wartortle

Take Your Breath Away

WARTORTLE HAS A LIFE SPAN OF UP TO 10,000 YEARS.

YOU LIVE FOR A REALLY LONG TIME, RIGHT, WARTORTLE?!

Quiz answer for page 73.

2

Squirtle strikes back with spouts of water at every opportunity.

Breath Holding Contest

NOW HOLD YOUR BREATH AS LONG AS YOU CAN!

THE PRIZE FOR THE WINNER IS A YEAR'S WORTH OF BERRIES! ♡

Nnngh...

KLICK

DOESN'T MATTER HOW LONG-LIVED I AM IF I PASS OUT FROM LACK OF OXYGEN!

What Pokémon category is Wartortle?

1 Shellfish Pokémon

2 Turtle Pokémon

3 Tiny Turtle Pokémon

No.
088
Central Kalos Pokémon

Blastoise

Lost in a Good Book

Pokémon Pocket Comics
HEH HEH... THIS POKÉMON POCKET COMICS BOOK IS SO-O-O-O FUNNY! ♡

bump
OW!

Quiz answer for page 75.
2

Wartortle is a Turtle Pokémon, Squirtle is a Tiny Turtle Pokémon and Blastoise is a Shellfish Pokémon.

HEY!
YOU HIT ME WITH YOUR ROCKET CANNON! WATCH WHERE YOU'RE GOING!

OH, FORGIVE ME! I'M TRULY SORRY!
smack
ARGH!

POKÉMON X•Y QUIZ

What does Blastoise's Ability change into when it Mega Evolves?

Mega Launcher

Drizzle

Iron Fist

No. 089
Central Kalos Pokémon

Skiddo

A Pokémon by Any Other Name

SKIDDIE, YOU'RE A REALLY LAID-BACK POKÉMON, AREN'T YOU?

Quiz answer for page 77.
1

Mega Blastoise's Ability is Mega Launcher, which boosts the power of Aura and Pulse moves like Water Pulse.

AND YOU'RE ALSO THE FIRST POKÉMON TO LIVE WITH HUMANS, ISN'T THAT RIGHT, SKIDDIE?

THE NAME ISN'T SKIDDIE, IT'S SKIDDO...

TALK TO YOU LATER, SKIDDIE!
BUT I DON'T LIKE CONFLICT, SO I'LL JUST SUFFER IN SILENCE.
DON'T MAKE THE SAME MISTAKE, EVERYONE!

POKéMON
X·Y
QUIZ

Skiddo, Binacle and Trubbish weigh the same. Which of them is the tallest?

1

Skiddo

2

Binacle

3

Trubbish

No. 090
Central Kalos Pokémon
Gogoat
A Great Way to Travel

YOU'RE SO COMFY TO RIDE ON! ♡
trot trot trot trot trot

Quiz answer for page 79.
1

I CAN READ YOUR THOUGHTS THROUGH MY HORNS...
...SO I KNOW WHICH WAY YOU WANT TO GO.

Skiddo is 2'11", Binacle is 1'08" and Trubbish is 2'00", so Skiddo is the tallest.

Urk

WHY DID YOU STOP? I THOUGHT YOU COULD READ MY THOUGHTS! I WANT TO KEEP GOING!

I KNOW YOU DO. BUT I DON'T WANT TO GET MY FEET DIRTY!

blorch

blorch

blorch

Gogoat compete to choose their leader by...

...running.

...jumping.

...clashing horns.

Central Kalos Pokémon No. 091

Pancham

Blame the Fault Lines

NO MATTER WHO PANCHAM'S OPPONENT IS, IT ALWAYS TRIES...
...TO LOOK AS TOUGH AS IT CAN.

Quiz answer for page 81.
3

Gogoat pick their leader through a battle of clashing horns.

WHAT'S WITH THAT STEELY GLARE, HUH?
YOU THINK I'M AFRAID OF YOU?
URK...

POKÉMON
X·Y
QUIZ

WHOA!

ARE WE HAVING AN EARTH-QUAKE ?!
MUST BE. YOU'RE SHAKIN' LIKE A LEAF.
wbbl
wbbl
wbbl
Try not to faint... Try not to faint...

Pancham attacks with Karate Chop. Which of the following Pokémon is it super effective against?

1

Weavile

2

Magikarp

3

Espurr

No.
092

Central Kalos Pokémon

Pangoro

Big Heart, Hard Head

HMM... THAT POKÉMON IS KINDA PUNY.

IT NEEDS SOMEONE TO LOOK OUT FOR IT.

Beware of Falling Ferroseed!

Quiz answer for page 83.
1

Fighting-type moves are super effective against Weavile, a Dark- and Ice-type Pokémon.

WHAT'S THIS...?
Beware of Falling Ferroseed!

HEY, BE CAREFUL! IT'S DANGEROUS TO GO THAT WAY!
Smak
?

ARE YOU TALKING TO ME...?
WHAT'S THAT ...?
klang
klang
klang
klang
THAT'LL TEACH ME NOT TO JUDGE A POKÉMON BY ITS SIZE...

POKÉMON X·Y QUIZ

Pangoro won't put up with bullying. What is its Pokémon type?

Fighting and Steel

Fighting and Rock

Fighting and Dark

No.
093

Central Kalos Pokémon

Furfrou

Cool or Clueless?

STYLING MY FUR NOT ONLY MAKES ME LOOK ELEGANT...
...IT INCREASES MY SWIFTNESS, TOO.

IN OTHER WORDS ...
I'M COOL! OH YEAH! ♡

Quiz answer for page 85.
3

Pangoro is a Fighting- and Dark-type Pokémon.

SO I PRACTICE...

...STANDING IN COOL POSES.

DON'T I LOOK MODEL-TASTIC LIKE THIS?

USING ME AS YOUR FOOTSTOOL IS TOTALLY ***NOT*** COOL!

What were Furfrou in the distant past?

Guardians of a king

Bodyguards on a ship

Spelunkers in caves

Central Kalos Pokémon No. 100

Scraggy

Next Time, Bring a Helmet

Quiz answer for page 87.

Historically, Furfrou guarded a king.

TALK ABOUT HARD-HEADED...
kwa flump

POKÉMON
XY
QUIZ

How does Scraggy protect itself when attacked? It...

...buries its body in the ground.

...pulls its skin up around its neck.

...counter-attacks with a head butt.

No.
101

Central Kalos Pokémon

Scrafty

Put on Your Best Face

SCRAFTY IS VERY POWERFUL.
I'M GONNA CRACK THIS ROCK IN TWO WITH JUST THE POWER OF MY VOICE!

Quiz answer for page 89.
2

Scraggy pulls its skin up around its neck to protect itself.

HIYAAA ...!
ting

Stomp
smak

kerrrak
k
WOW! YOU CRACKED THAT ROCK IN TWO WITH JUST THE POWER OF YOUR *NOSE*! ♡

POKéMON
X Y
QUIZ

Scrafty choose their group leader based on...

1

...the power of its kick.

2

...the loudness of its voice.

3

...the size of its crest.

No. 104
Central Kalos Pokémon
Mega Alakazam
The Nap Master

MEGA ALAKAZAM LEVITATES WHILE MEDITATING.

Quiz answer for page 91.
3

Scrafty choose their group leader based on how big its crest is.

IT MUST BE EXHAUSTING TO STAY UP IN THE AIR LIKE THAT FOR SO LONG!
WHY DON'T YOU RELAX FOR A WHILE?
I AM RELAXED!

YAAWWWNN...

IF YOU SAY SO... ZZZZZ...
BUT MAYBE NOT *THAT* RELAXED...

POKÉMON X•Y QUIZ

What does the red organ on Mega Alakazam's forehead do?

Emits psychic power

Creates super-sonic sound

Shoots out laser beams

No. 106
Central Kalos Pokémon
Gloom
Smell

I LOVE THE SMELL OF DIRT ON MY FINGERS AFTER I WORK IN MY GARDEN...
YOU DO?!
Sniff
Sniff

Quiz answer for page 93.
1

The red organ on Mega Alakazam's forehead emits psychic power.

THEN MAYBE YOU'LL LIKE THE WAY GLOOM SMELLS TOO.
GO ON! TAKE A WHIFF!
Come on! Give it a try!

ONLY ONE IN A THOUSAND LIKE GLOOM'S SCENT...
Snnniiiiffff

fwump
AND *THEY* NEED SERIOUS HELP...

POKÉMON
XY
QUIZ

What does the nectar oozing out of Gloom's mouth smell like?

Super sweet

Wonderfully refreshing

Atrociously stinky

Central Kalos Pokémon
No. 114
Espurr
Ear Ear!

ESPURR IS ALWAYS SO ALOOF...

Quiz answer for page 95.
3

IT ACTS LIKE IT'S THE ONLY POKÉMON IN THE WORLD!

Gloom's drool is an atrocious-smelling, nose-curling nectar that can be detected from more than a mile away.

IT'S FOLDING ITS EARS DOWN NOW...
SO IT DOESN'T HAVE TO LISTEN TO US!

NO! I'M NOT FOLDING MY EARS TO AVOID YOU...
SHFF
I'M FOLDING MY EARS TO AVOID *MYSELF*...
IT HEARD US?!
BUT... HOW?!
ESPURR KEEPS ITS INTENSE PSYCHIC POWER IN CHECK BY KEEPING ITS EARS DOWN.

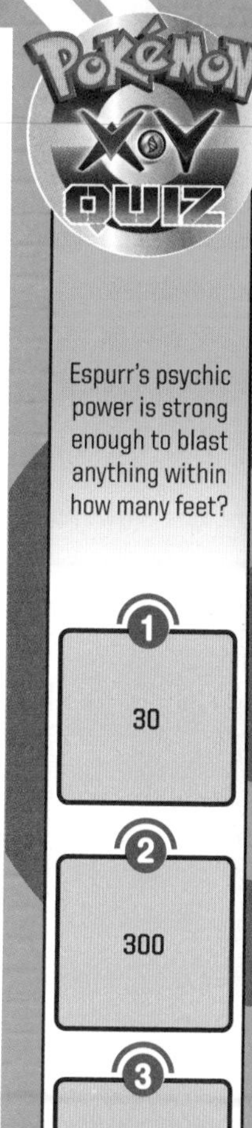
POKÉMON
X Y
QUIZ
Espurr's psychic power is strong enough to blast anything within how many feet?
1
30
2
300
3
3,000

No. 115

Central Kalos Pokémon

Meowstic

Hide-and-Seek the Easy Way

THE EYE-SHAPED PATTERNS INSIDE MEOWSTIC'S EARS EMIT EXTREME PSYCHIC POWER.
MEOWSTIC HIDES THE PATTERNS BECAUSE THEIR POWER IS TOO INTENSE.

READY? SET?
YEP! COME AND GET ME! ♪

Quiz answer for page 97.

2

Espurr's psychic power is strong enough to blast anything within 300 feet.

shff

Aaaah!
NO FAIR USING YOUR EARS!
I'LL NEVER BE ABLE TO HIDE FROM YOU!
wOOOOOPf
ffffft
POWER SOURCE

What Pokémon category is Meowstic?

Psychic Pokémon

Constraint Pokémon

Restraint Pokémon

Central Kalos Pokémon

No.
117

Honedge

Get the Hilt?

HELP ME!

GRAB MY HILT!
Sword hilt
SURE...

Quiz answer for page 99.

2

Meowstic is a Constraint Pokémon. Espurr is an example of a Restraint Pokémon.

HONEDGE'S BLUE CLOTH STRAP WRAPS AROUND THE ARM OF ANYONE WHO DARES TO GRAB THE HILT OF ITS SWORD-SHAPED BODY.
AND THEN... IT DRAINS THE UNLUCKY VICTIM'S LIFE ENERGY.
Wrap
Wrap
Hee hee hee...

WHAT'S SO FUNNY?
YOU'RE FALLING OFF THE CLIFF WITH ME.
I'M WHAT ...?!

POKéMON
X·Y
QUIZ

Honedge's Ability is No Guard. What kind of Ability is it?

Its defense is zero, but its attack is doubled.

The opponent's defense becomes zero, but its attack is doubled.

All attacks used by or against Honedge can't miss.

No. 118
Central Kalos Pokémon
Doublade
Double Trouble

WHEN HONEDGE EVOLVES, IT DIVIDES INTO TWO SWORDS TO BECOME DOUBLADE.
DOUBLADE TALKS TO ITSELF VIA TELEPATHY.

Quiz answer for page 101.
3

No Guard is an Ability that enables all attacks used by or against it to hit its target.

HEY, OTHER BLADE!
WHAT IS IT, OTHER BLADE?

MY BACK ITCHES!
MY BACK ITCHES!
WE HAVE THE SAME BACK!

YOU SCRATCH IT. I DON'T WANT TO!
SO SCRATCH IT ALREADY!
IF YOU WON'T DO IT, I WON'T EITHER!
THEIR ARGU-MENTS NEVER END.

POKéMON X·Y QUIZ

What Pokémon category is Doublade?

Sword Pokémon

Blade Pokémon

Cooperation Pokémon

Central Kalos Pokémon

Aegislash

Once and Future King

AEGISLASH RECOGNIZES THOSE DESTINED TO BECOME ROYALTY.
HM...
I CAN TELL THAT...

Quiz answer for page 103.

1

Doublade is a Sword Pokémon.

...THAT POKÉMON WILL BECOME A KING SOMEDAY!
This one here

WHAT DO YOU WANT TO BE WHEN YOU GROW UP, CHESPIN?
OH, THAT'S EASY...
A KING, RIGHT?!

A RAMEN-NOODLE CHEF!
pwump
AEGISLASH DID NOT SEE THAT COMING.

What Pokémon category is Aegislash?

Sword Pokémon

Royal Sword Pokémon

Royal Pokémon

Central Kalos Pokémon

Spritzee

Stop and Smell the Spritzee

YOU SMELL SO NICE, SPRITZEE.

Quiz answer for page 105.
2

Aegislash is a Royal Sword Pokémon.

DO I? YOU KNOW, MY SCENT CHANGES...
...DEPENDING ON WHAT I EAT!

OOH... EAT SOME SPICY CURRY THEN!
RAMEN NOODLES!
SALISBURY STEAK! ♡
PUSH

fwapfwap
AT LEAST THEY AREN'T SUGGESTING CABBAGE. OR BRUSSELS SPROUTS.

POKÉMON
X·Y
QUIZ

Spritzee, Floette and Chingling are the same height. Which of them is the heaviest?

1

Spritzee

2

Floette

3

Chingling

No. 130

Central Kalos Pokémon

Aromatisse

Silent but Deadly

BE CAREFUL, EVERYONE!
AROMATISSE ATTACKS WITH A HORRIBLE STENCH!

Wafffft
UGH...
WAIT... THAT SMELLS LIKE...

Quiz answer for page 107.

2

Spritzee is 1.1 lbs., Floette is 2.0 lbs. and Chingling is 1.3 lbs. So Floette is the heaviest.

...CURRY?!

YOU'RE MAKING ME HUNGRY!
grmmbl
NO FAIR!
HEH HEH... I CAN ATTACK WITH GOOD SMELLS TOO! ♡

POKÉMON
X Y
QUIZ

What Pokémon category is Aromatisse?

1

Perfume Pokémon

2

Scent Pokémon

3

Fragrance Pokémon

No. 131
Central Kalos Pokémon

Swirlix

Sweet Tooth

SWIRLIX LOVES TO EAT SWEETS.

Quiz answer for page 109.
3

Aromatisse is a Fragrance Pokémon. Spritzee is a Perfume Pokémon.

TRY THIS SWEET BERRY, SWIRLIX.
Ooooh, thanks!

WANT SOME MORE?
WHY ARE YOU GIVING ALL YOUR BERRIES TO THAT POKÉMON?!

BECAUSE SWIRLIX IS SO FLUFFY AND CUTE! ♡
YOU'RE SWEET ON SWIRLIX, AREN'T YOU?

POKéMON
X Y
QUIZ

To entangle its opponents, Swirlix extrudes sweet and sticky white...

1. ...threads.

2. ...cotton candy.

3. ...powder.

No. 132
Central Kalos Pokémon
Slurpuff
Traitor

sniff sniff
HUH?
THERE'S A TRAITOR AMONG US...

Quiz answer for page 111.
1

THAT'S IMPOSSI-BLE!
WHAT ?!
BOOOO!

Swirlix extrudes white threads that are sweet and sticky to entangle its opponents.

THE FOUR OF US TOOK A SOLEMN OATH...
...NOT TO BREAK OUR DIETS!

IT'S VERY FAINT, BUT I SMELL ***CHOCOLATE***!
NO WAY! I ONLY ATE ONE LITTLE PIECE THREE DAYS AGO!
snff snff
snff snff

POKÉMON X·Y QUIZ

Slurpuff can distinguish the faintest of scents. How much stronger is its sense of smell compared to humans?

1 million times

10 million times

100 million times

Central Kalos Pokémon No. 139

Snorlax

Best Place to Nap

SNORLAX SAID IT WAS SLEEPY, SO...
...I TOLD IT TO GO SLEEP ON THE RAIL!
WHAT?

ZZZZZZZ
BUT THE TRAIL STARTS AT THE BRIDGE!
SNORLAX WILL BLOCK THE WAY IF IT LIES DOWN THERE!

Quiz answer for page 113.

3

Slurpuff's sense of smell is 100 million times better than a human's.

I THINK YOU MISHEARD ME. WE WON'T HAVE A PROBLEM WALKING ACROSS THE BRIDGE.

OF COURSE WE WILL WITH SNORLAX LYING ON IT! LET'S GO LOOK, AND I'LL PROVE IT TO YOU!

ZZZZ ZZZ
Rail
Bridge
SNORLAX
OHHHH... YOU SAID "RAIL," NOT "TRAIL." I THOUGHT THAT WAS JUST A TYPO.

POKÉMON
X·Y
QUIZ
How many pounds of food does Snorlax eat every day?
1
8
2
88
3
880

No.
144

Central Kalos Pokémon

Mega Medicham

An Arm-y of Arms

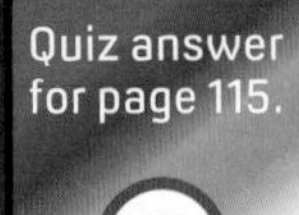
3

Quiz answer for page 115.

Snorlax doesn't feel full unless it eats 880 lbs. of food a day.

LOOK! ♪

MY FOUR EXTRA ARMS LOOK SO REAL AND LIFELIKE, DON'T THEY? ♫

BUT YOU ALREADY HAVE TWO ARMS. YOU DON'T NEED MORE.
SURE I DO!

Pokémon
X Y
QUIZ

WITH THESE ARMS...
...I CAN GET READY MUCH FASTER IN THE MORNING! ♡
KLICK
BRUSH TEETH
TURN ON TV
CLEAN UP
COOK BREAKFAST

Mega Medicham's unique characteristic is its four independent arms. What are they made of?

Enhanced willpower

Underworld energy

Solar energy beams

No.
145

Central Kalos Pokémon

Zubat

Never Saw It Coming

HOW CAN YOU FLY SO FAST WITHOUT EYES?
ZWIP
ZWIP
And in the dark too!

I'VE NEVER BUMPED INTO ANYTHING IN MY WHOLE ENTIRE LIFE! ♪
EASY. I SENSE MY SURROUNDINGS BY BOUNCING ULTRASONIC WAVES OFF OF OBJECTS.
Whee! ♡

Quiz answer for page 117.
1

Mega Medicham's four arms are created out of its enhanced willpower.

HEY! THERE'S A GHOST RIGHT BEHIND YOU!
WHAT ?!
krash

SO YOU DO BUMP INTO THINGS AFTER ALL.
THAT DOESN'T COUNT!

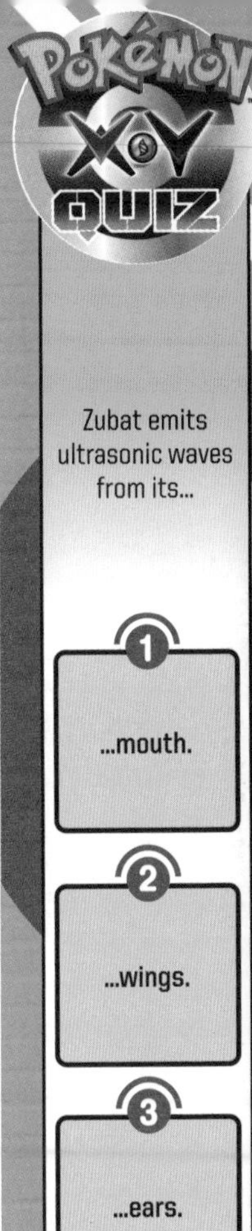
POKÉMON X•Y QUIZ
Zubat emits ultrasonic waves from its...
1
...mouth.
2
...wings.
3
...ears.

Coastal Kalos Pokémon

Zangoose

Lovestruck

Zubat's mouth emits ultrasonic waves.

HUH? ZANGOOSE AND SEVIPER ARE FACING OFF, BUT... THEY AREN'T FIGHTING?

OH, I GET IT... THEY'RE SHOWING OFF FOR SYLVEON.

Pokémon
X Y
QUIZ

BUT AS SOON AS SYLVEON LEAVES...
Bye!

What is Zangoose's greatest weapon?

Pointy fangs

Lightning that shoots out of its mouth

Sharp claws

SYLVEON LIKES *ME* BEST!
Are you kidding ?!
...THE BATTLE BEGINS.
...

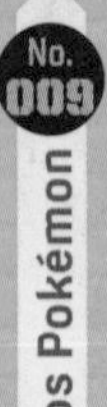
No.
009

Coastal Kalos Pokémon

Mega Absol

Show-Off, Not Liftoff

CAN YOU FLY, MEGA ABSOL?
NOPE.

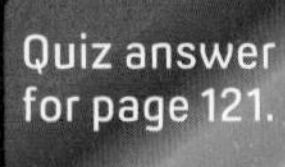

Quiz answer for page 121.

3

When Zangoose is mad, it gets up on its hind legs and extends its claws.

THEN HOW COME YOU HAVE WINGS?
DUNNO. THEY JUST APPEAR WHEN I MEGA EVOLVE.

SO... THEY'RE USE-LESS?
NAH. THEY'RE VERY USEFUL.

THEY MAKE ME POPULAR.
Ooh, how beautiful!
So fluffy!
SIGH... I WANT TO MEGA EVOLVE TOO!
Vip

POKÉMON X•Y QUIZ

Which of its qualities doesn't change after Absol Mega Evolves?

1. Ability
2. Height
3. Weight

No.
010

Coastal Kalos Pokémon

Inkay

Bait and Switch

HERE'S A WORD OF ADVICE FROM A VETERAN...
HEY, ROOKIE ...!
OH, HELLO, TENTA-COOL...

Quiz answer for page 123.
2

Mega Absol's height doesn't change.

...WILL APPEAR IN THE SEA IN FRONT OF YOU.
plop
SOME-TIMES TASTY FOOD...
Yeah, just like that.
BUT IT'S A TRAP! NEVER, EVER TRY TO EAT IT LIKE THIS...

yaaannnnk
Aaaaah!
blub blub blub blub
SEE WHAT I MEAN ...?!
UM...

WHY, YES. I MOST CERTAINLY DO.

POKéMON
XY
QUIZ

What does Inkay do when it is attacked?

1

Dances around wildly

2

Spurts ink on its opponent

3

Flashes the lights on its body

No.
011
Coastal Kalos Pokémon

Malamar

No Time for Nap Time

SO... SLEEPY...
MALAMAR MUST BE USING HYPNOSIS ON ME!

Quiz answer for page 125.
3

Inkay flashes the light-emitting spots on its body to drain its opponent's will to fight.

OHHH...
CAN'T...FIGHT IT... GOOD NIGHT... EVERYBODY...
...

DON'T LOOK AT ME!
I DIDN'T DO ANYTHING!
I KNOW.

CUT IT OUT, CHESPIN! QUIT PRETENDING YOU'RE ASLEEP!
FINISH YOUR HOME-WORK!
And don't try to pin it on me!
GULP!
twitch

POKÉMON
X Y
QUIZ

What does Malamar do after luring its prey over using its powerful hypnosis?

1. Wraps its tentacles around its prey

2. Blinds its prey with light

3. Breathes fire on its prey

No. 013
Coastal Kalos Pokémon
Solrock
Hard to Read

SOLROCK IS EXPRESSIONLESS.

Quiz answer for page 127.
1

Malamar wraps its tentacles around its prey before finishing it off with its digestive juices.

YOU CAN'T TELL WHAT IT'S FEELING.
BUT IT HAS THE ABILITY TO READ OTHERS' EMOTIONS.
...

YOU'RE GREEDY.
HUH?!
lub dub

YOU'RE HIDING SOMETHING BEHIND YOUR BACK, AREN'T YOU?
OKAY, OKAY! YOU CAN HAVE ONE TOO. SHEESH...
YOU DIDN'T *LOOK* HUNGRY!

POKÉMON
X Y
QUIZ

What happens when Solrock spins around?

It gives off light.

Its energy increases.

It shoots laser beams.

Coastal Kalos Pokémon No. 015

Shelgon

Pick Up After Yourself

SHELGON'S SHELL BREAKS OFF THE INSTANT IT BEGINS TO EVOLVE.
twitch
OH WOW! I'M GOING TO EVOLVE! YAY!

shatter
I've evolved into Salamence! Yahoo!
krak

Quiz answer for page 129.

1

When Solrock spins around, its body lights up.

thump
stub

OWW! OUCH!
WHO LEFT THESE HARD SHELLS LYING AROUND ON THE GROUND?!
UH... THAT WOULD BE *YOU*...

POKÉMON X·Y QUIZ
Shelgon's shell is very...
1
...light.
2
...heavy.
3
...sweet.

Coastal Kalos Pokémon

No.
021

Binacle

Who Did It?

HUP!
jump

Quiz answer for page 131.
2

Shelgon's shell is very heavy, so it moves sluggishly.

OH NO!
ker-splash

WE LANDED IN THE PUDDLE BECAUSE YOU WOULDN'T JUMP WITH ME!
WHAT?!
OH, IT'S ALL *MY* FAULT AGAIN?!
THAT DOES IT! I'M MOVING TO A DIFFERENT ROCK!

krash
WHOA! GOOD THING I MOVED US HERE!
AND THEN THEY BEGIN TO FIGHT OVER WHO SAVED WHOM...

POKÉMON
X Y
QUIZ

What does Binacle eat?

Magikarp

Bog moss

Seaweed

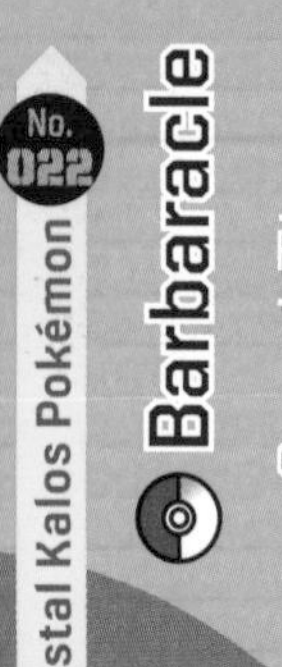

No. 022
Coastal Kalos Pokémon
Barbaracle
Celebrate Good Times

I HEARD YOU WON ANOTHER BATTLE!
HEY, BARBAR-ACLE!

Quiz answer for page 133.
3

IT WAS NOTHIN'.
AW...

Binacle eats seaweed that washes up on the shore.

I JUST GOT LUCKY, IS ALL.
NOTHIN' TO BRAG ABOUT.
BARBARACLE'S FACE LOOKS SO HUMBLE...

...BUT ITS ARMS AND LEGS ARE HAVING A DANCE PARTY!

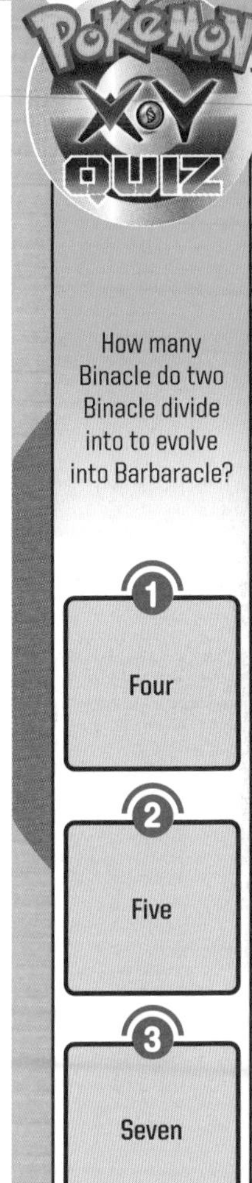
POKÉMON
X·Y
QUIZ
How many Binacle do two Binacle divide into to evolve into Barbaracle?
1
Four
2
Five
3
Seven

No. 025
Coastal Kalos Pokémon
Tentacool
Bait Bait and Switch Switch

GREETINGS, ROOKIE! SO WE MEET AGAIN...
OH, HI, TENTA-COOL!

Quiz answer for page 135.
3

Barbaracle is made up of two Binacle that divide into seven Binacle.

TODAY, I'M GONNA INTRODUCE YOU TO MY BUDDY TENTACRUEL!
WELCOME TO THE SEA!
HELLO!

PLOP
PLOP
OH...
UM...

YANK YANK
THEY SURE HAVE A LOT IN COMMON...
BUBBL BUBBL

POKÉMON
X Y
QUIZ

Which of the following is true about Tentacool?

1

It lives deep in the sea.

2

Its body is composed almost entirely of water.

3

It glows when wet.

No. 030
Coastal Kalos Pokémon
Skrelp
Rotten to the Core

HEY, SKRELP!
DO YOU STINK WHEN YOU GO ON LAND?

Quiz answer for page 137.
2

Tentacool's body is composed almost entirely of water.

DO I STINK?!
YOU'RE ROTTEN, RIGHT?

I ONLY *PRETEND* TO BE ROTTEN KELP!
DON'T YOU KNOW WHAT "PRETEND" MEANS, DUMMY?!
OH, I SEE...

I CAN'T BELIEVE HOW STUPID HORSEA IS!
CAN YOU BELIEVE WHAT HORSEA ASKED ME...?
WHAT AN ANNOYING, SCATTER-BRAINED, PUNY...
frzzl
frzzl
frzzl
IN SOME WAYS, YOU REALLY *ARE* ROTTEN...

POKÉMON
X·Y
QUIZ

Skrelp is camouflaged as rotten kelp. How does it catch its prey?

1. By spraying poison on it

2. By paralyzing it with electricity

3. By catching it with its tail and fins

Coastal Kalos Pokémon

Dragalge

Keep Our Seas Beautiful

blurb blurb
OH NO! ANOTHER SINKING SHIP!
THIS AREA MUST BE HOME TO A LOT OF DRAGALGE.

Quiz answer for page 139.
1

Skrelp sprays poison on its prey.

SPLISH
WHAT DO YOU EXPECT?
THEY'RE TRESPASSING IN OUR BACKYARD! AND FRONT YARD. AND SIDE YARD...

No Trespassing!
WHY DON'T YOU JUST PUT UP A "NO TRESPASSING" BUOY?
That should warn seafarers off.

THEY COULD JUST LOOK IN ANOTHER DIRECTION. IT'S THE SAME VIEW ALL AROUND...
blub blub
SIGNS MESS UP OUR VIEW. ♡
pffsss

POKéMON X•Y QUIZ

Skrelp is a Poison- and Water-type Pokémon. What is Dragalge's Pokémon type?

Poison and Dragon

Water and Dragon

Poison and Water

No.
032

Coastal Kalos Pokémon

Clauncher

All In

CLAUNCHER'S SIGNATURE MOVE IS CRABHAMMER...
...AN ATTACK WITH A HIGH CRITICAL-HIT RATIO.

Quiz answer for page 141.
1

Dragalge is a Poison- and Dragon-type Pokémon.

kerrash

Eeeeek...
fsss...
fsss...
fsss...
YAAA-AHHHH!!!

SORRY, SORRY!
I GOT A LITTLE CARRIED AWAY...
IT'S JUST...
...A CARD GAME!

Clauncher shoots compressed water out of its claw. What target does it shoot at?

Swimming prey

Diving prey

Flying prey

No. 033
Coastal Kalos Pokémon
Clawitzer
A Weighty Matter

LET'S SEE... I WEIGH... 15.4 POUNDS!
WANT TO WEIGH YOURSELF TOO, CLAWITZER?
SCALE

Quiz answer for page 143.
3

Clauncher shoots down flying prey.

trip
CLAWITZER CAN'T BALANCE ON THE SCALE BECAUSE OF THE WEIGHT OF ITS OVERSIZED CLAW.

JUST GIMME A SEC TO—OOF!—GET ON THE SCALE.
SO? HOW MUCH DO I WEIGH?
...

UM...
ACTUALLY, I CAN'T TELL.

POKÉMON X•Y QUIZ

The speed of ships is measured in knots, which are equivalent to 1.15 mph. How fast can Clawitzer move?

20 knots

40 knots

60 knots

No. 046
Coastal Kalos Pokémon
Helioptile
A Light Snack

I GENERATE ENERGY THROUGH PHOTOSYNTHESIS BY BASKING IN SUNLIGHT.
SO I DON'T NEED TO EAT FOOD.

Quiz answer for page 145.
3

Clawitzer can swim at 60 knots.

WOW!
MUNCH MUNCH MUNCH
THAT'S AMAZING! THIS SURE TASTES GOOD, THOUGH...
...

HEY, UM...
MIND IF
I HAVE
ONE...?
NO
WAY!

YOU EAT ***LIGHT***.
WHAT A
WEIRD
DIET...
BUT IT'S
CLOUDY
TODAY!
SIGH...

POKÉMON
X·Y
QUIZ

Helioptile uses Quick Attack. Which of the following Pokémon is it not effective against?

1

Honedge

2

Diggersby

3

Inkay

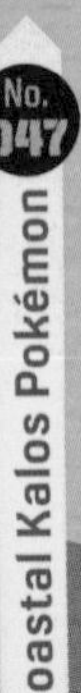
No. 047
Coastal Kalos Pokémon

Heliolisk

With a Little Prodding

HURRY UP OR WE'LL BE LATE FOR THE SHOW!
I'M RUNNING AS FAST AS I CAN!

Quiz answer for page 147.
1

Quick Attack is a Normal-type move. It doesn't have any effect on Honedge because it is a Ghost-type Pokémon.

CHESPIN IS SO-O-O-O SLOW.

AIYEE !!
ZZZt

IF I STIMULATE MY MUSCLES WITH ELECTRICITY, I CAN RUN 100 YARDS IN FIVE SECONDS.
YOU CAN! IT DOESN'T WORK THAT WAY WITH *ME*! *YEOWCH*!
ACTUALLY, LOOKS LIKE IT DOES...

POKÉMON X·Y QUIZ

How does Heliolisk create electricity?

With generator cells on the side of its head

With its tail

By flaring its frills

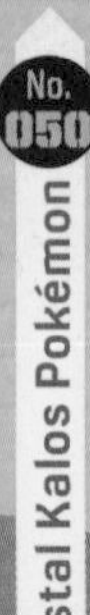
No. 050
Coastal Kalos Pokémon

Rhyhorn

The Straight and Narrow

WHOA! THAT ROAD LOOKS ROUGH AND ROCKY...

Quiz answer for page 149.
3

Heliolisk flares its frills to generate electricity.

HEY, RHYHORN!
WOULD YOU MIND GIVING ME A RIDE? ♡
HUH?! OH, SURE...

Pokémon
X Y
QUIZ

THIS IS THE LIFE! TRAVELING IN COMFORT AND STYLE!
ARE YOU SURE ABOUT THIS...?

RHYHORN ALWAYS RUNS IN A STRAIGHT LINE.
kerrrassh

What Pokémon category is Rhyhorn?

Spikes Pokémon

Brutal Pokémon

Charging Pokémon

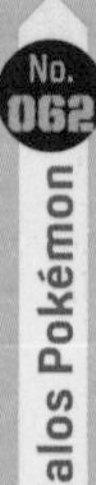

Coastal Kalos Pokémon

Mega Kangaskhan

A Manner of Speaking

bmp

No. 062
Quiz answer for page 151.
1

Rhyhorn is a Spikes Pokémon.

HEY! AREN'T YOU GONNA APOLOGIZE FOR BUMPING INTO ME?!
I'LL TAKE CARE OF THIS, MOM!

A LITTLE BRAT LIKE YOU?!
YOU'RE GOING TO FIGHT KROOK-ODILE?!
READY ...? SET ...?

WE WEREN'T PAYING ATTENTION! PLEASE DON'T EAT US! PRETTY PLEASE, WITH SUGAR ON TOP?
UM...
LET'S JUST CONSIDER THIS MATCH A FORFEIT...

POKéMON X•Y QUIZ

Mega Kangaskhan's Ability changes after it Mega Evolves. What else changes?

1. Its weight

2. Its height

3. Nothing

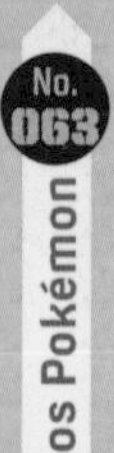
No.
063

Coastal Kalos Pokémon

Mega Mawile

Always Brush Your Hair...Er...Teeth

YOU SHOULD DO THIS YOURSELF!

Quiz answer for page 153.
1

IT WAS HARD ENOUGH WITH ***ONE***... BUT NOW I'VE GOT ***TWO***!
PUH-LEASE?!

When Kangaskhan Mega Evolves, its weight changes from 176.4 lbs. to 220.5 lbs.

OKAY, FINE...

brush brush

brush brush

brush brush

I HAVE TO TAKE CARE OF THEM OR I'LL GET CAVITIES IN MY EARS!

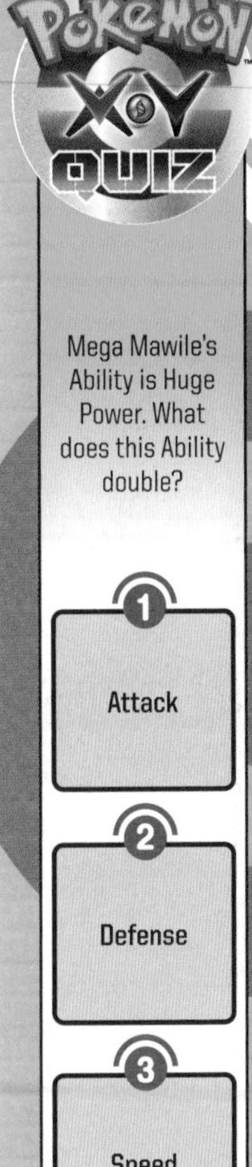

POKéMON X·Y QUIZ
Mega Mawile's Ability is Huge Power. What does this Ability double?
1
Attack
2
Defense
3
Speed

Coastal Kalos Pokémon

Tyrunt

Soft and Chewy on the Inside

DOESN'T THIS FLAN LOOK TASTY?!
LOOK! ♡

Quiz answer for page 155.
1

Huge Power doubles Mega Mawile's attack.

HOW CAN SOFT AND GOOEY FLAN TASTE GOOD?
NAH. I LIKE MY FOOD CRUNCHY.

I'LL PUT IT IN THE FRIDGE...
...AND SAVE IT FOR TOMOR-ROW. ♪

THE NEXT DAY...
WHERE DID MY FRIDGE GO?!
YOU WERE RIGHT! IT TASTED GREAT WITH A CRUNCHY SHELL! ♡

POKéMON
X Y
QUIZ

Tyrunt attacks with Dragon Tail. Which of the following Pokémon is it super effective against?

1
Dedenne

2
Dragalge

3
Doublade

No. 065
Coastal Kalos Pokémon
Tyrantrum
Full Speed A-head

HEY.
I CHALLENGE YOU TO FIGHT ME HEAD-TO-HEAD!
HUH? OKAY! ONE, TWO...

Quiz answer for page 157.
2

ker-thunk

Dragon-type moves are super effective against Dragon-type Pokémon. Dragalge is a Poison- and Dragon-type Pokémon.

HUH?
WHERE'D YOU GO?!

!
twtch twtch
NEXT TIME, LET'S FIGHT MANO A MANO...

POKÉMON X•Y QUIZ
With its powerful jaw, Tyrantrum can shred thick metal plates like paper. What is its Ability?
1 Intimidate
2 Strong Jaw
3 Rock Head

No.
066

Coastal Kalos Pokémon

Amaura

A Mighty Calm Wind

I'VE HEARD THAT AMAURA IS A VERY CALM POKÉMON.

Quiz answer for page 159.
2

Tyrantrum's ability is Strong Jaw.

CALM ABOUT WHAT, I WONDER...
?

OoooPS...
...
poot

TEE HEE.
grin
CALM ABOUT FARTING...?!

Amaura was restored from a part of its body that was frozen in ice for how many years?

3 million

50 million

100 million

No. 067
Coastal Kalos Pokémon

Aurorus

A Chilling Welcome

HEY, TYRANTRUM! LONG TIME NO SEE! YOU LOOK SO CHILL YOU'RE GOING TO FREEZE-DRY!

ARGH!

Quiz answer for page 161.
3

Amaura was frozen in ice for over 100 million years.

krak
krek
krik

HUH...? DID I FREEZE SOLID BECAUSE THAT JOKE WAS SO BAD...
...OR BECAUSE OF MY FREEZE-DRY MOVE?
PROBABLY BOTH.

Pokémon X·Y Quiz

Aurorus, Tyrantrum and Xerneas have gathered together. Which of them is the heaviest?

1

Aurorus

2

Tyrantrum

3

Xerneas

No. 068
Coastal Kalos Pokémon

Mega Aerodactyl

Keep Your Chin Up

HEH HEH... I'M SO FAST THAT I CAN ATTACK BEFORE MY OPPONENT DOES!
I'M GOING TO BE DEFEATED BEFORE I GET TO USE ANY MOVES!

Quiz answer for page 163.
2

At 595.2 lbs., Tyrantrum is the heaviest. Aurorus weighs 496.0 lbs., and Xerneas weighs 474.0 lbs.

MWAHA-HAHAHA! LOOKS LIKE...
...I'VE SEIZED THE INITIATIVE IN THIS BATTLE!

grab

BUT I'VE SEIZED YOUR *CHIN*!
grab

POKéMON
X·Y
QUIZ

What increases when Aerodactyl Mega Evolves?

Its attack

Its speed

Its defense

No. 074

Coastal Kalos Pokémon

Mega Manectric

Roll with the Punches

I LIKE TO CURL INTO A BALL AND...
...ROLL!

Quiz answer for page 165.
2

Aerodactyl's speed increases when it Mega Evolves.

I LIKE TO CREATE LIGHTNING AND...
...MAKE **THUNDER** ROLL!

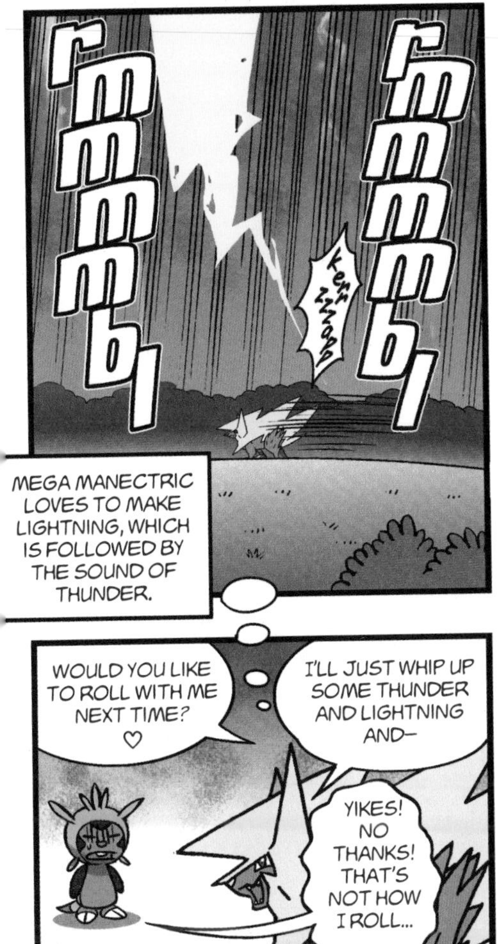

rmmmmbl

kerrzzzapp

rmmmmbl

MEGA MANECTRIC LOVES TO MAKE LIGHTNING, WHICH IS FOLLOWED BY THE SOUND OF THUNDER.

I'LL JUST WHIP UP SOME THUNDER AND LIGHTNING AND—

WOULD YOU LIKE TO ROLL WITH ME NEXT TIME? ♡

YIKES! NO THANKS! THAT'S NOT HOW I ROLL...

Mega Manectric's Ability is Intimidate. What does this Ability do to its opponent?

Lowers its attack

Puts it to sleep

Paralyzes it

No. 076

Coastal Kalos Pokémon

Mega Houndoom

A Little Pun with Friends

WE'RE BFF'S, RIGHT, MEGA CHARIZARD Y?

WE ARE?

Quiz answer for page 167.

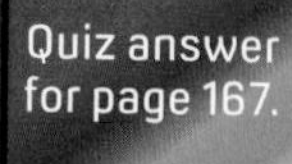

1

Intimidate lowers Mega Manectric's opponent's attack by one stage.

BECAUSE YOU AND I HAVE GOOD CHEMISTRY.
Chemistry?

BUT WHY THAT
IS CERTAINLY IS
A CHE-MYSTERY!
GET IT?
DO YOU?
AHAHAHAHA...

NOPE. WE ARE NOT BFF'S. NOPETY NOPE NOPE.
flap flap
I COULD NEVER BE FRIENDS WITH SOMEONE WHO DOESN'T APPRECIATE A BRILLIANT PUN ANYWAY!

POKéMON
X·Y
QUIZ

Why are Mega Houndoom's claws dark red?

Because they generate more heat

To make a fashion statement

To kick more strongly

Coastal Kalos Pokémon

No. 085

Sylveon

Peace, Love and Pudding

SYLVEON'S RIBBONLIKE FEELERS...
...RADIATE A SOOTHING AURA.

Quiz answer for page 169.
1

AHH... MMM... SIGH...
MY ANGER... IS GRADUALLY... FADING AWAY...
WUMWUMWUM

Mega Houndoom's claws are dark red because they generate more heat than before it Mega Evolved.

I DON'T EVEN REMEMBER...
...WHAT I WAS ANGRY ABOUT! ♡

BUT LATER THAT NIGHT, CHESPIN REMEMBERS.

GUESS WHAT? I ATE THE FLAN IN YOUR FRIDGE, CHESPIN.
You did what?!
Do you mind? ♡
boing

POKÉMON X·Y QUIZ

Sylveon, who lives in the Kalos region, is the latest of Eevee's final evolutions. How many evolutions does Eevee have?

1. Six
2. Eight
3. Ten

Coastal Kalos Pokémon
No. 089
Hawlucha
Diving for Comfort

Hyyurgh!

Quiz answer for page 171.
2

Sylveon is Eevee's eighth and final form so far.

ta-tump
YAAA-ARGH!

FLYING PRESS!
flap flap

SO... SOFT... ♡
♡
FWUMP
HAWLUCHA SURE LOVES ITS NEW BED... THE OLD ONE MUST HAVE BEEN MADE OF ROCKS! OR NAILS!

POKÉMON X·Y QUIZ

Hawlucha is a Fighting- and Flying-type Pokémon. What Pokémon category is it?

Flying Pokémon

Battle Pokémon

Wrestling Pokémon

No. 098
Coastal Kalos Pokémon
Sawk
Insomnia

SAWK WANTS TO PERFECT ITS STRONGEST ATTACK.
Punch
Punch

Quiz answer for page 173.
3

Hawlucha is a Wrestling Pokémon.

SO IT'S TRAINING WITHOUT EVEN TAKING A BREAK TO SLEEP.
Hyungh!
Smash
Smash
Hyungh!
Smash
Yahhhh!

PANGORO WATCHES SAWK TRAIN...
...ALL NIGHT LONG...

STOP IT!
I CAN'T SLEEP EITHER WITH ALL THOSE PUNCHING NOISES YOU'RE MAKING!
GLARE
You're softer than this rock. If I punched **you**, it wouldn't be so noisy...

POKéMON
X Y
QUIZ

When Sawk ties its belt, which of its actions becomes more powerful?

1

Punches

2

Kicks

3

Head butts

No. 110
Coastal Kalos Pokémon
Dedenne
Socket to Me

HEY! THE TV WON'T TURN ON!
IT'S A WASTE OF ELECTRICITY TO WATCH TV SO MUCH.

Quiz answer for page 175.
1

BE MORE ECO-FRIENDLY. ♪
YOU SHOULD CONSERVE ENERGY.

Tying its belt gets Sawk pumped up and makes its punches more powerful.

AWWW...
OOOOH... ♡
SAVING ENERGY IS VIRTUOUS.
HEY! GET YOUR TAIL OUTTA MY ELEC-TRICAL SOCKET!

POKÉMON X•Y QUIZ

Dedenne absorbs electricity from electric sockets and shoots it out from which part of its body?

Ears

Whiskers

Tail

No. 124
Coastal Kalos Pokémon
Carbink
Quizzical

QUIZ TIME!
WHAT'S MY FAVORITE SHOE?!

Quiz answer for page 177.

2

BOOTS ...?
SAN-DALS ...?
HIGH HEELS ...?

Dedenne fires electricity out of its whiskers.

BZZZTT... ♪
YOU'RE ALL WRONG! I DON'T WEAR SHOES! ♡

WE'RE OUTTA HERE.
Umm...
OH!
WAIT!
PLEASE COME AGAIN!
Why do my visitors always leave so soon...?

POKÉMON X•Y QUIZ

For how many years has Carbink been sleeping underground?

Hundreds

Thousands

Hundreds of millions

No. 125
Tauros
Tail Tells
Coastal Kalos Pokémon

REMEMBER, YOU CAN TELL WHEN TAUROS IS ABOUT TO CHARGE BY ITS TAIL.
THE MOMENT TAUROS'S TAIL STARTS WHIPPING BACK AND FORTH, WE'D BETTER RUN FOR THE HILLS!
GOT IT!

Quiz answer for page 179.
3

Carbink has been sleeping underground for hundreds of millions of years.

Whp whp
NOW!!

POKÉMON
X Y
QUIZ

RUN ...!!
dash

SOMETIMES I'M JUST SCRATCHING AN ITCH, YOU KNOW...
whp whp

What Pokémon category is Tauros?

Tail Pokémon

Bullfight Pokémon

Wild Bull Pokémon

No.
129

Coastal Kalos Pokémon

Mega Ampharos

An Unwelcome Surprise

ONE DAY I'M TAKING A STROLL,
AND ALL OF A SUDDEN...

Quiz answer for page 181.
3

Tauros is a Wild Bull Pokémon.

BOO!!
AIIEEEE

MEGA GENGAR FRIGHTENS ME SO BADLY...

...IT SCARES THE IRIS RIGHT OUT OF MY EYES!

POKÉMON X•Y QUIZ

Mega Ampharos turns into an Electric- and Dragon-type Pokémon. What else about it changes?

1 Its Ability

2 Its weight

3 Its height

No.
130

Coastal Kalos Pokémon

Mega Pinsir

Even Mega Pokémon Have Allergies

rub
rub

Quiz answer
for page 183.
1

WHAT'S WRONG,
MEGA PINSIR...?
rub
rub
rub

Mega Ampharos's Ability changes from Static to Mold Breaker.

I'VE GOT MEGA ITCHY EYES!
shffff

THAT'S NOT A PUNCH LINE, JOKE OR PUN...!
Nope. It's just annoying to me.

When Pinsir Mega Evolves into Mega Pinsir, what type does it become?

Bug

Bug and Dragon

Bug and Flying

No.
131

Coastal Kalos Pokémon

Mega Heracross

A Flat-tering Portrait

Skrbbl
skrbbl

Skrbbl
skrbbl

Quiz answer for page 185.
3

Mega Pinsir is a Bug- and Flying-type Pokémon.

I DREW PIKACHU.
YOU DREW WHO?!

LOOKS MORE LIKE A MEGA SCRIBBLE...
Everybody's a critic!

When Mega Heracross unleashes its maximum power, its...

...temperature rises.

...body swells up.

...horn grows.

No. 145
Coastal Kalos Pokémon
Octillery
Octillery Artillery

lub dub
lub dub
lub dub
lub dub

Quiz answer for page 187.
1

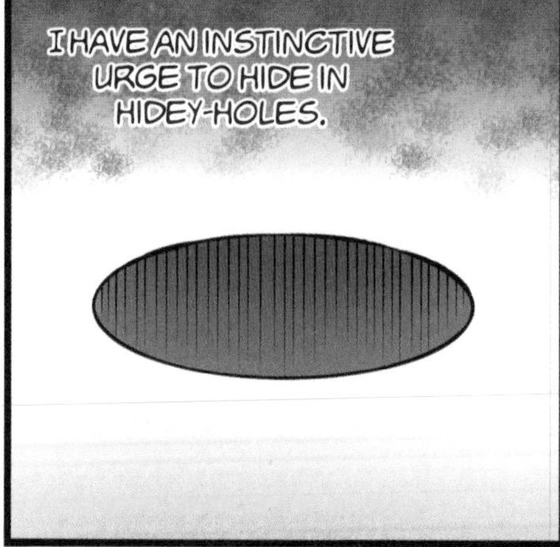
I HAVE AN INSTINCTIVE URGE TO HIDE IN HIDEY-HOLES.

When Mega Heracross unleashes its maximum power, its body temperature rises dramatically, so it opens the shells of its arms and torso to let the excess heat escape.

fooomp

BUT **THIS** ONE WASN'T THE BEST CHOICE!

What Pokémon category is Octillery?

Rock Head Pokémon

Hole Hiding Pokémon

Jet Pokémon

No. 008
Mountain Kalos Pokémon

Mega Garchomp

A New Use for New Powers

SO WHAT'S DIFFERENT ABOUT YOU...
...NOW THAT YOU'VE MEGA EVOLVED?
WELL, FOR ONE THING, GET A LOAD OF MY NEW ARM BLADES!

THEY'RE MUCH BIGGER THAN BEFORE, AREN'T THEY?!
Gwa ha ha ha!
I'M INCREDIBLY POWERFUL NOW! ♡

Quiz answer for page 189.
3

Octillery is a Jet Pokémon.

REALLY ?
SHOW ME!
YOU GOT IT! ♡
Whff
Whff
Whff

OOOHHH... THAT FEELS NICE...
Like a really great set of fans!
HEY!
They're for battling!
NOT AIR-CONDI-TION-ING!

POKÉMON
X Y
QUIZ

What changes when Garchomp Mega Evolves into Mega Garchomp?

1

Its Ability

2

Its height

3

Its weight

Mountain Kalos Pokémon

Goomy

I'm Gonna Gitcha, Goomy!

Swap
slipp

Quiz answer for page 191.

1

Garchomp's Ability changes from Sand Veil to Sand Force.

slipp
Swap

CAN'T... GET UP... ONE MORE TIME...
I GIVE UP! THANKS FOR A GREAT BATTLE!
I lost.
huff
huff
huff

GUESS WHAT? I'M THE WEAKEST OF ALL THE DRAGON-TYPE POKÉMON!
PLEASE TELL ME YOU'RE LYING...

POKÉMON
X·Y
QUIZ

Where does Goomy live?

Humid swamps

Damp, shady places

Freezing snowcapped mountains

No. 020
Mountain Kalos Pokémon

Sliggoo

See What I Did There?

SLIGGOO HAS EYES, BUT THEY HAVE DEVOLVED, SO IT DOESN'T USE THEM.

Quiz answer for page 193.
2

INSTEAD IT USES ITS FOUR HORNS...
...TO SENSE ENEMIES, TO HEAR SOUNDS... AND EVEN TO SMELL.

Goomy lives in damp, shady places so that its slimy body won't dry out.

SLIGGOO...
...IF I WORE YOU ON MY FEET, WOULD YOU BE A SLIGSHOE?
grin

?
LOOKS LIKE THOSE HORNS OF YOURS CAN'T SENSE A GOOD PUN THOUGH, HUH?

POKÉMON X•Y QUIZ

Sliggoo attacks its opponents with what kind of attack?

Punching them with its horns

Grabbing them with its slimy body

Excreting a sticky liquid that dissolves anything

No. 021
Mountain Kalos Pokémon

Goodra

Slip, Sliming Away

Splorch
Splorch
Splorch
I LOVE YOU, GOODRA! ♪

Now I'm all slimy!
Perfect!

Quiz answer for page 195.

3

Sliggoo attacks by excreting a sticky liquid that can dissolve anything.

SEE YA TOMORROW!
jump
shfffpp

NOW I CAN SLED DOWN THIS HILL! THIS IS EVEN BETTER THAN ROLLING DOWN IT!
Shhhhhhsssss
Hurray!

POKéMON
X·Y
QUIZ

Goodra uses which part of its body to attack?

Its retractable horns

Its slimy body

A sticky liquid that dissolves anything

No. 029
Mountain Kalos Pokémon
Carnivine
A Cliché Come True

OOOH, WHAT A HUGE, YUMMY-LOOKING BERRY!

Quiz answer for page 197.
1

munch
munch
IT TAKES CARNIVINE A WHOLE DAY TO EAT A LARGE BERRY.

Goodra attacks with its retractable horns, throwing punches with the force of a hundred pro boxers.

Pokémon
X•Y
QUIZ

THE NEXT DAY...

Argh!
I DISLOCATED MY JAW!
THAT'S WHAT YOU GET FOR BITING OFF MORE THAN YOU CAN CHEW!

How does Carnivine entrap its prey?

By opening its large mouth and waiting

With its sweet-smelling saliva

By using Poison Dance

No. 032
Mountain Kalos Pokémon
Mega Gengar
Get the Picture?

OH! THERE'S MEGA GENGAR!

Quiz answer for page 199.
2

Carnivine attracts its prey with its sweet-smelling saliva.

MAY I TAKE A PICTURE OF YOU?
GO AHEAD. ♡

FLASH

AWW... YOUR EYES WERE CLOSED!
NOT THE ONE ON MY FORE-HEAD!
You're supposed to keep all your eyes open.

POKÉMON X•Y QUIZ

What can Mega Gengar see with its third unblinking eye?

1 The future

2 The past

3 Other dimensions

No.
050
Mountain Kalos Pokémon
Klefki
Lost and Lost

!

Quiz answer for page 201.
3

OH! JYNX DROPPED A KEY ON THE GROUND. I SHOULD HELP OUT...

It is said that Mega Gengar's third eye can see into other dimensions.

There we go!
Hey, I lost that key!
TRASH
If I meant to throw it in the trash, I wouldn't have missed!

POKÉMON
X Y
QUIZ

Klefki is a Key Ring Pokémon. What is its Pokémon type?

Steel and Flying

Steel and Fairy

Steel and Ghost

Mountain Kalos Pokémon

Phantump

A Berry Strong Hint

HEY THERE!

Quiz answer for page 203.

2

Klefki is a Steel- and Fairy-type Pokémon.

WANT ME TO PLACE THE CURSE OF THE FOREST ON YOU? HUH? DO YOU?
UH... NO THANK YOU!

THEN YOU'D BETTER...
...BE *VERY* NICE TO ME...

RIGHT! I GET IT! HERE! TAKE THE *NICE BERRY*!
...*VERY, VERY NICE*!
GLARE

POKÉMON
XY
QUIZ

Phantump are stumps possessed by the spirit of what...?

Banette

Animals

Children

No. 062
Mountain Kalos Pokémon

Trevenant

A Wooden Celebration

Hurray!
YAHOO! ♪
I WON MY BATTLE! ♡

Quiz answer for page 205.
3

silence...
...
THERE'S NO ONE HERE TO CONGRATULATE ME...

Phantump are stumps possessed by the spirits of children lost in the forest.

TREVENANT HAS THE POWER TO CONTROL THE TREES IN THE FOREST.

CONGRATULATIONS TO ME!

WAY TO GO, ME!

wave wave

wave wave

♡

BUT...
Sigh
...IT'S JUST NOT THE SAME...

POKÉMON
XY
QUIZ

Trevenant won't forgive anyone who harms the forest. But it is kind to others. Who?

1

Pokémon who live in the forest

2

Pokémon who live in its branches

3

Spirits lost in the forest

No. 063
Mountain Kalos Pokémon
Pumpkaboo
One Size Doesn't Fit All

LET'S EAT! ♡
YES, LET'S! ♡
PUMPKABOO COME IN FOUR DIFFERENT SIZES.

Quiz answer for page 207.
2

Trevenant is kind to Pokémon who live in its branches.

THAT WAS GOOD! ♡
Hasn't finished yet
munch munch

I'M STILL HUNGRY...
Still hasn't finished.
munch munch
munch munch

I'M SO JEALOUS! THE BERRIES WE ATE WERE THE SAME SIZE, BUT I'M BIGGER!
I'll save some for later
Drool

POKÉMON X•Y QUIZ

Pumpkaboo is a Pumpkin Pokémon. When is it active?

1

At the break of dawn

2

In the afternoon

3

At sunset

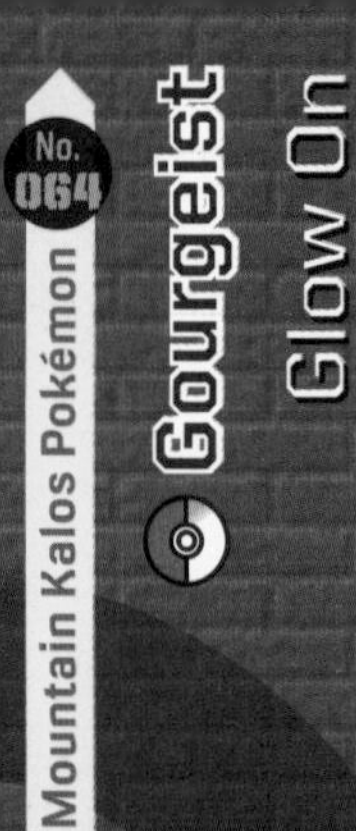
No. 064
Mountain Kalos Pokémon
Gourgeist
Glow On

PUMPKABOO JUST EVOLVED INTO GOURGEIST.

Quiz answer for page 209.
3

WOW, GOURGEIST!
YOU'RE SO PRETTY NOW THAT YOU'VE EVOLVED! YOU HAVE A SPECIAL GLOW ABOUT YOU...
HUH?! WHAT ARE YOU TALKING ABOUT ?!

Pumpkaboo becomes restless and active at sunset.

THAT'S RUDE.
SORRY... I MEANT IT AS A COMPLI-MENT.

I'M GOURGEIST, SO I'M NOT *PRETTY*, I'M *GORGEOUS*!
YOU ARE *PETTY* THOUGH...

POKéMON
X Y
QUIZ

When does Gourgeist wander the world singing an eerie song?

1

On the night of a new moon

2

On the first day of the month

3

On the last day of the month

No. 079
Mountain Kalos Pokémon
Bergmite
Punny Contest

BERGMITE, WHAT'S YOUR POKÉMON CATEGORY?
Brrr! It's so cold where you live!
shvvr
shvvr
shvvr
ICE CHUNK POKÉMON.

Quiz answer for page 211.
1

OH. *ICE-SEE*!
UHH... DID CHESPIN COME ALL THIS WAY JUST TO MAKE THAT PUN?!

Gourgeist sings in an eerie voice and wanders the streets on the night of the new moon.

I'M GOOD AT PUNS TOO!
LISTEN TO THIS! I'M AN ICE-TYPE POKÉMON, SO... I'M REALLY ***COOL***!

FINE. YOU WIN.
And I came all this way in the cold...
I'M OUTTA HERE.
SHIVVY
SHIVVY
N-ICE SEEING YOU! ♡

POKÉMON X•Y QUIZ

Bergmite blocks its opponents' attacks with the ice that shields its body. What happens when it cracks?

It repairs itself right away.

It divides into two Bergmite.

It faints.

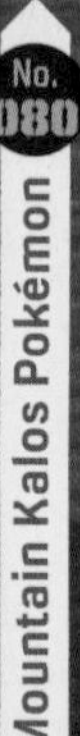
No. 080
Mountain Kalos Pokémon

Avalugg

To Have and Too Cold

Quiz answer for page 213.

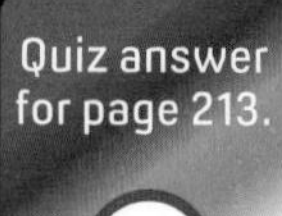
1

Bergmite uses cold air to quickly repair its cracks with new ice.

YOU'RE COLD ?!
WHAT ?!

WE'RE ICE-TYPE POKÉMON! WE CAN'T ADMIT TO THAT!
WHERE'S YOUR PRIDE?!

MAYBE I LOST IT WHEN I CAUGHT THIS COLD...?

toss
YOU IDIOT!
DON'T TAKE IT OUT ON ME! CHILL OUT, WILL YOU?!

POKéMON
XY
QUIZ

Steelix, Wailord and Avalugg have gathered together. Which of them is the heaviest?

1. Steelix

2. Wailord

3. Avalugg

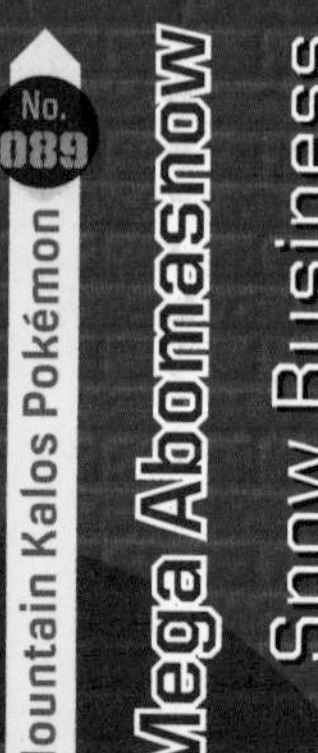
No. 089
Mountain Kalos Pokémon
Mega Abomasnow
Snow Business

MAYBE IT'S BECAUSE OF MY JAGGED BODY THAT...

Quiz answer for page 215.
3

Wailord is 877.4 lbs., Steelix is 881.8 lbs. and Avalugg is the heaviest at 1113.3 lbs.

HUP...!
roll roll roll
...WHENEVER I ROLL AROUND...

...I TURN INTO A SNOWBALL.
...

LUCKILY, I CAN SHAKE THE SNOW OFF NO PROBLEM!
platch
platch
platch
roll roll
OH YEAH? WELL NOW YOUR NO PROBLEM IS MY PROBLEM!

POKéMON
X Y
QUIZ

What is Mega Abomasnow's Pokémon type?

Rock and Ice

Grass and Ice

Ice and Water

No. 101
Mountain Kalos Pokémon
Mega Aggron
DIY

Quiz answer for page 217.
2

Mega Abomasnow is a Grass- and Ice-type Pokémon.

WE'LL HAVE TO CHECK THE MAP NOW. DO YOU MIND...?
KRCK!

KRCK

Map of Cave

YOU MAKE A GREAT CANDELABRA! ♡

Mega Aggron can turn a steel-clad tank into scrap metal. What is its Pokémon type?

Steel

Steel and Rock

Steel and Dragon

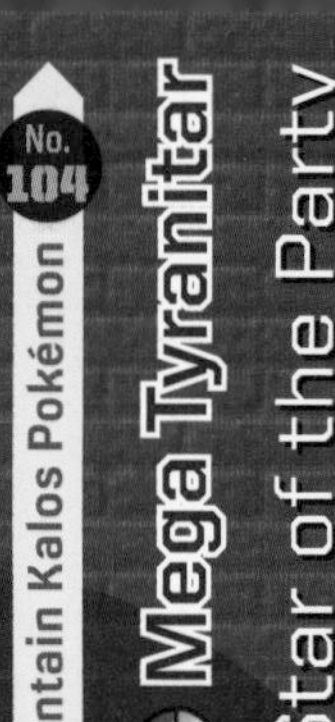
No. 104
Mountain Kalos Pokémon
Mega Tyranitar
Star of the Party

AH, THERE YOU ARE!
WOULD YOU COME WITH ME, PLEASE...?

Quiz answer for page 219.
1

Mega Aggron is a Steel-type Pokémon.

THIS WAY... A LITTLE FARTHER... ♪
FWIP FWIP
?

WOULD YOU MIND WEARING THESE FOR A FEW DAYS?!
?!

MERRY CHRIST-MAS!
...
MERRY CHRISTMAS! THANKS, MEGA TYRANITAR! OUR CHRISTMAS PARTY WOULDN'T BE THE SAME WITHOUT YOU!

POKéMON
X Y
QUIZ

What is inside the red part of Mega Tyranitar's torso?

1

Fire

2

Immense energy

3

Poisonous fluid

No. 113
Mountain Kalos Pokémon
Noibat
Too Energetic

YOUR ULTRASONIC WAVES ARE AMAZING!
THEY'RE A FORM OF ENERGY WE CAN'T SEE WITH OUR EYES, RIGHT?
Uh-huh! ♥

Quiz answer for page 221.

2

The red part of Mega Tyranitar's torso is seething with energy.

LIKE THE BEAMS THAT COME OUT OF THIS REMOTE CONTROL FOR MY TV.
Too bad it's out of batteries...
NOT REALLY. NOT EVEN CLOSE.

WATCH!
?

Can a remote do this?!
krashh
AGH! I JUST WANTED YOU TO CHANGE THE CHANNEL FOR ME!

POKÉMON X•Y QUIZ

Noibat's 200,000-hertz ultrasonic waves would make even a huge wrestler dizzy. Where are they emitted from?

Its mouth

Its ears

Its wings

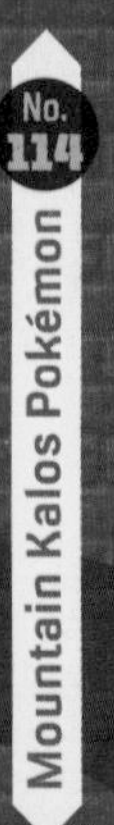
No. 114
Mountain Kalos Pokémon

Noivern

Not Kept in the Dark

NOIVERN CAN...
...FLY AROUND SWIFTLY IN THE DARK...
SWIP
WIP

Quiz answer for page 223.
2

...SO IT OFTEN TRAVELS AT NIGHT.
!

Noibat emits ultrasonic waves from its enormous ears.

URK!
I'M ON A DIET! AND NOIVERN JUST CAUGHT ME SNEAKING A MIDNIGHT SNACK!

PLEASE DON'T TELL THE OTHERS!
Jynx, Azumarill, Slurpuff and I are dieting together.
I won't breathe a word.
ON ITS TRAVELS, NOIVERN OFTEN DISCOVERS SECRETS HIDDEN FROM THE LIGHT OF DAY.

POKéMON
X Y
QUIZ

Noivern is ferocious and difficult to defeat in the dark. What calms it down?

1 Licking flower nectar

2 Hanging out with Noibat

3 Eating fruit

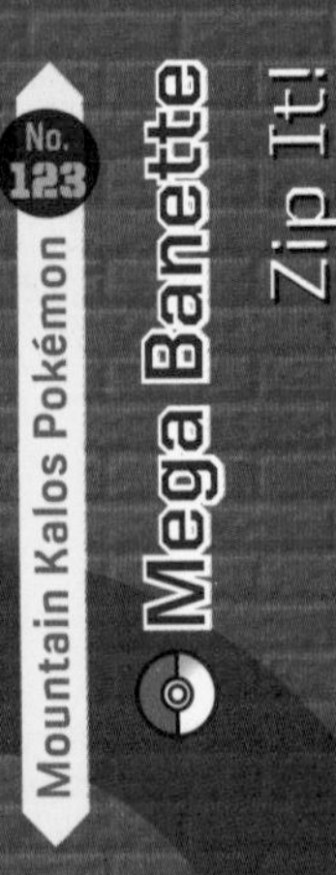

No. 123
Mountain Kalos Pokémon
Mega Banette
Zip It!

GOOD MORNING, MEGA BANETTE! ♪

Quiz answer for page 225.
3

HEY! IT'S RUDE NOT TO RETURN A GREETING!
MMPH.
MM-MMPH.
OH, RIGHT... YOU CAN'T SPEAK BECAUSE YOUR MOUTH IS ZIPPED SHUT.

Noivern loves fruit and calms down when it eats some.

WHY DON'T YOU UNZIP IT?
GOOD IDEA!

MISCHIEF SUCCESSFUL! ♡
WHO CLOSED MY HAND ZIPPERS?!

POKéMON
X Y
QUIZ

Mega Banette's Ability is Prankster. What does it do?

Increases the priority of a status move

Doubles an attack

Increases the move's chances of a critical hit

No. 137

Mountain Kalos Pokémon

Mega Scizor

Steel Yourself for This One

I AM MEGA SCIZOR!
I'M A BUG- AND STEEL-TYPE POKÉMON, SO I HAVE AN ADVANTAGE AGAINST FAIRY-TYPE POKÉMON!

Quiz answer for page 227.
1

The Prankster Ability increases the priority of a status move.

LIAR...
WHAT ...?!
HOW DARE YOU! I NEVER LIE!

YOU CALL YOURSELF A STEAL-TYPE POKÉMON...
...BUT YOU DIDN'T TAKE ANY OF MY STUFF!
EMPTY
HUH...?! I'M NOT A STEAL-TYPE POKÉMON...
...I'm a Steel-type Pokémon!

What type of Pokémon is Mega Scizor, to be exact?

Flying and Steel

Bug and Steel

Steel

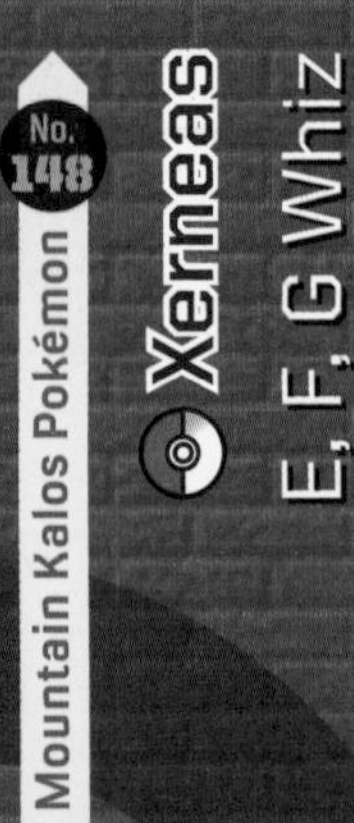
No. 148
Mountain Kalos Pokémon
Xerneas
E, F, G Whiz

I WANT TO LEARN GEOMANCY TOO!
BUT ONLY I CAN USE THAT MOVE.

Quiz answer for page 229.

2

I DON'T BELIEVE IT! I'M SURE I CAN LEARN IT IF I TRAIN REALLY HARD!
sha

Mega Scizor is a Bug- and Steel-type Pokémon.

A, B, C, D, E, F, G... WOW. THIS MATH STUFF IS HARDER THAN I THOUGHT...
MATH STUFF?

YOU KNOW, THESE LINES AND TRIANGLES AND CIRCLES...
YEAH.
That kind of thing.
YOU MEAN GEOMETRY?! *THAT'S* THE *ALPHABET*!

What is the name of Xerneas's unique Ability that increases damage from Fairy-type moves?

Pixilate

Fairy Guard

Fairy Aura

No. 149
Mountain Kalos Pokémon
Yveltal
Glowing Mad

YVELTAL HAS BEGUN TO GLOW RED!

Quiz answer for page 231.
3

Xerneas's Ability is Fairy Aura.

RUN!
ZOOOOM

WHAT MADE YVELTAL SO MAD?
WHAT'S HAPPEN-ING?
WHO CARES?! JUST RUN!

I'm so annoyed!
I FORGOT TO RECORD MY FAVORITE TV SHOW!
EVEN LEGENDARY POKÉMON NEED TO LEARN TO NOT SWEAT THE SMALL STUFF.

POKÉMON X•Y QUIZ

What is the name of Yveltal's unique Ability that increases damage from Dark-type moves?

1

Dark Aura

2

Black Aura

3

Break Aura

Mountain Kalos Pokémon

Zygarde

Never-Ending Mission

YOU ALWAYS STAND SO STILL, ZYGARDE... WHY IS THAT?

I'M KEEPING AN EYE ON THINGS.
LIKE WHAT...?

Quiz answer for page 233.

1

Yveltal's unique Ability is Dark Aura.

OH, I SEE! WHAT WILL YOU DO WHEN YOU CATCH THEM IN THE ACT?
PEOPLE WHO DESTROY THE ECOSYSTEM, FOR EXAMPLE.

UH... OKAY. WELL... KEEP ON KEEPING ON!
...
CONTINUE TO MONITOR THEM.

POKÉMON
X Y
QUIZ

Zygarde is an Order Pokémon. What type of Pokémon is it?

1

Dragon and Dark

2

Dragon and Fairy

3

Dragon and Ground

No. 151
Mountain Kalos Pokémon
Mega Mewtwo X
A Glassy Stare

MEGA MEWTWO X IS A PSYCHIC- AND FIGHTING-TYPE POKÉMON...
...AS YOU CAN SEE BY ITS RIPPLING MUSCLES.
WHOO-HOO!
CHECK OUT MY BULGING BICEPS! ♡

Quiz answer for page 235.
3

Zygarde is a Dragon- and Ground-type Pokémon.

HRR-NGH...

Hrrr rrngh!
rppl rppl
HRRRR-RNGH!

MEGA MEWTWO X SPENDS A LOT OF TIME IN FRONT OF THE MIRROR.
I AM SO COOL I CAN HARDLY STAND IT! ♡
UM... YOU MISSED YOUR BATTLE...

Pokémon
X Y
QUIZ

Mega Mewtwo X's Ability is Steadfast. What is its type?

Dark and Fighting

Psychic and Fighting

Steel and Fighting

Mountain Kalos Pokémon

No. 151

Mega Mewtwo Y

Y the New Look for Mewtwo?

slam
ALL RIGHT!
TIME TO HEAD OUT TO BATTLE!

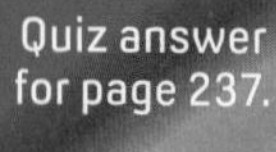

Quiz answer for page 237.

2

Mega Mewtwo X is a Psychic- and Fighting-type Pokémon.

yank

WHY DID MY HEAD HAVE TO GROW SO **LONG** WHEN I MEGA EVOLVED...?!
ARGH! NOT AGAIN!

Wrap wrap
HUH? IS THAT A FASHION STATE-MENT?!
Or another form change ?!
...

THANK YOU FOR READING ALL THE WAY TO THE END! HOPE YOU HAD A LOT OF PUN!

Pokémon Pocket Comics

Story & Art by SANTA HARUKAZE

English Adaptation/Bryant Turnage, Annette Roman
Translation/Tetsuichiro Miyaki
Touch-up & Lettering/Susan Daigle-Leach
Design/Shawn Carrico
Editor/Annette Roman

Printed in China

Published by VIZ Media, LLC
P.O. Box 77010
San Francisco, CA 94107

10 9 8 7 6 5 4 3
First printing, December 2016
Third printing, October 2017

viz
media

viz.com

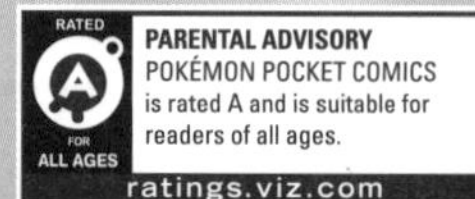
RATED
A
FOR
ALL AGES
PARENTAL ADVISORY
POKÉMON POCKET COMICS
is rated A and is suitable for
readers of all ages.
ratings.viz.com